The Justice Master

The rediscovered cases of Sherlock Holmes Book 6

Arthur Hall

Copyright © Arthur Hall 2021

The right of Arthur Hall to be identified as the author of this work has been asserted by him in accordance with the Copyright, Designs and Patents Act 1998.

All rights reserved. No reproduction, copy or transmission of this publication may be made without express prior written permission. No paragraph of this publication may be reproduced, copied or transmitted except with express prior written permission or in accordance with the provisions of the Copyright Act 1956 (as amended). Any person who commits any unauthorised act in relation to this publication may be liable to criminal prosecution and civil claims for damage.

All characters appearing in this work are fictitious or used fictitiously. Except for certain historical personages, any resemblance to real persons, living or dead, is purely coincidental. The opinions expressed herein are those of the author and not of MX Publishing.

Paperback 978-1-78705-752-4
ePub ISBN 978-1-78705-753-1
PDF ISBN 978-1-78705-754-8

MX Publishing
335 Princess Park Manor, Royal Drive,
London, N11 3GX
www.mxpublishing.com

Cover design by Brian Belanger
www.belangerbooks.com and *www.redbubble.com/people/zhahadun*

Arthur Hall was born in Aston, Birmingham, UK, in 1944. His interest in writing began during his schooldays and served as a growing ambition to become an author.

Years later, his first novel 'Sole Contact' was an espionage story about an ultra-secret government department known as 'Sector Three' and has been followed, to date, by five sequels.

Other works include five 'rediscovered' cases from the files of Sherlock Holmes, two collections of bizarre short stories and two novels about an adventurer called 'Bernard Kramer', as well as several contributions to the ongoing anthology, 'The MX Book of New Sherlock Holmes Stories'.

His only ambition, apart from being published more widely, is to attend the premier of a film based on one of his novels, ideally at The Odeon, Leicester Square.

He lives in the West Midlands, United Kingdom, where he often walks other people's dogs as he attempts to formulate new plots.

His work can be seen at: arthurhallsbooksite.blogspot.com, and the author can be contacted at: arthurhall7777@aol.co.uk

By the same author:

The 'Sector Three' series:
Sole Contact
A Faint and Distant Threat
The Final Strategy
The Plain Face of Truth
A Certain Way to Death
The Suicide Chase

The 'Bernard Kramer' series:
The Sagittarius Ring
Controlled Descent

Volumes of fantastic short stories:
Facets of Fantasy
Curious Tales

Rediscovered cases from the files of Sherlock Holmes:
The Demon of the Dusk
The One Hundred per Cent Society
The Secret Assassin
The Phantom Killer
In Pursuit of the Dead
Further Little-Known Cases of Sherlock Holmes
Tales From the Annals of Sherlock Holmes

CONTENTS

Chapter 1	A Visit From Inspector Lestrade	1
Chapter 2	Mr Latimer Causes Delay	10
Chapter 3	The Unexpected Victim	24
Chapter 4	The Buccaneer	39
Chapter 5	Loose Ends Are Dangerous	55
Chapter 6	A Trap is Set	66
Chapter 7	A Narrow Escape	77
Chapter 8	Carpenters Mews and After	95
Chapter 9	The Next Victim	108
Chapter 10	Plantain Castle	121
Chapter 11	Lestrade Closes the Case	137

Chapter 1 - A Visit From Inspector Lestrade

When my friend Mr Sherlock Holmes had established himself in his chosen profession of consulting detective, it was perhaps inevitable that his path would cross often with that of Scotland Yard. I can recall more than a few instances when his advice would be sought by the likes of Inspectors Lestrade, Gregson and Hopkins, among others, but none when he was unable or unwilling to assist their official enquiries.

Indeed, there were occasions when the Yard had become impatient with its own lack of progress and, having many other unsolved cases to pursue, discontinued or reduced its current investigation although the file remained open. One of these, in particular, remains uppermost in my mind so that, subject to my friend's permission, I am able to refer to my notes of the time and disclose the tale to the public by means of my publisher.

Breakfast having been concluded, we sat in our armchairs with the pale light of an early autumn morning illuminating our sitting-room.

"We have a visitor I think, Holmes," I said, lowering my newspaper.

"Doubtlessly it is Inspector Lestrade. His usual sequence of repeated rings of the door-bell is unmistakeable."

"You are correct, for I heard his voice. Mrs Hudson precedes him on our stairs at this very moment."

Holmes laid his copy of *The Standard* aside. "He probably seeks my advice on the Barrington case. Had he consulted me before, the affair would have been over a week ago."

I was about to ask him to elaborate when, after a sharp rap on the door, it opened to admit our landlady. "Inspector Lestrade to see you, Mr Holmes."

"Thank you, Mrs Hudson," he acknowledged. Then, after the inspector entered and greetings had been exchanged, "Would you like tea, Lestrade?"

Our visitor, breathing heavily, declined politely and our landlady withdrew. I relieved him of his hat and coat and indicated that he should be seated in the basket chair. The seasonal coolness had necessitated that the fire be lit, and it crackled merrily in the grate as he settled himself.

Holmes regarded the inspector, who appeared to be experiencing some indecision, with interest.

"Well Lestrade, I perceive that you are here to relate to me a tale. Not the Barrington case after all, I think. It will be something that the Yard is having difficulty with, for your expression tells me that you are struggling with your pride. I know how the official force is reluctant to admit failure, but I'll wager that it is a situation more uncommon these days."

The inspector appeared to take heart from the somewhat veiled encouragement that my friend offered, and began to explain his presence haltingly.

"It's true, Mr Holmes, that there are less unsolved cases than before, but what gets my goat is when an investigation is shelved because the Assistant Commissioner thinks that we are progressing too slowly or that newer crimes seem to him to be more important."

"I can imagine your frustration, when you have already invested many hours to no end. You have, I trust, a particular instance in mind?"

"Indeed, sir, I have."

A faint smile crossed Holmes' face "I take it then, that there is a case that you have been ordered to abandon, and that you do so reluctantly. It concerns something about which you feel strongly, and you wish me to advise you or pursue it in your stead?"

Our visitor scrutinized the pattern on the carpet at his feet. "I do not like to see murderers escape justice, Mr Holmes. Not for any reason."

"Nor do I." My friend reached for his old briar and began to stuff it with coarse tobacco from the Persian slipper that he had placed near at hand. "Perhaps the best thing would be for you to enlighten us as to the details, and then we can decide what is to be done."

Lestrade glanced at me, and I nodded my approval.

"Thank you, gentlemen. I confess to being deeply concerned. There are in fact no less than six murders unsolved, beginning in January of last year with Mrs Martha Berryfield. The following April saw Mr Raymond Tarwill as the next victim. Then came Mr Thomas Leroy in November, and Miss Grace Lightwell and Mr Donald Rearden a few months later in February. Finally, Mr Roger Carvell met his end in May."

Holmes blew out a fragrant stream of smoke. "And you have reason to believe that the killer of each of these is the same? Is there then, a common link?"

"There is, Mr Holmes, and it was obvious quite early in my investigation. It is also, I suspect, why my superiors have discontinued my enquiries with so little regard."

"Pray share it with us."

I saw that Holmes' interest was aroused, for his eyes glittered. We both leaned forward in our chairs so as to miss nothing of Lestrade's explanation.

"Every one of those victims, without exception, was released from prison shortly before their demise and after serving a sentence for a capital crime."

"Extraordinary. Some sort of revenge crusade, perhaps." Holmes suggested.

"That was one of my first considerations. Unfortunately, the enquiry led nowhere."

"That is unfortunate. I assume you have brought more details with you?"

"Indeed, sir." Lestrade produced his notebook from his pocket.

"You were confident then, that I would agree to assist you." My friend smiled again after knocking out his pipe and placing it aside.

"We are no longer newly acquainted, Mr Holmes. I have come to know something of your ways, and to appreciate your methods."

"Quite so. Watson, kindly take up your own notebook and write down the salient points from what the inspector has to tell us."

I complied instantly and, after riffling through the pages, Lestrade began:

"In January of last year, Mrs Martha Berryfield was released from Holloway. She had spent less than a year of a life sentence for poisoning her husband after suspecting, wrongly it seems, that he had begun a friendship with another woman. As it happens, the woman in question was the wife of Viscount Ferrersly, who would have none of this since he trusts his wife absolutely. It was, in fact, the Viscount, curiously enough, whose influence caused the death sentence of Mrs Berryfield first to be commuted, and then to be quashed on appeal. Shortly after her release, Mrs Berryfield was found strangled near her home."

I think my thoughts must have been apparent from my expression. Lestrade looked at me strangely, but my friend understood at once.

"Watson does not approve of the rich and powerful manipulating justice for their own ends," Holmes explained.

"Nor do I," the little detective responded, "but it is the way of the world."

"Quite, but pray continue."

"During the following April," the inspector resumed, "A certain Mr Raymond Tarwill, the owner of a glass-eye manufacturing concern, was acquitted of murdering his business partner by pushing him in front of a speeding carriage. He was able to employ the highly-skilled defence solicitor, Mr Timothy Quirk-Rollason, who apparently showed reasonable doubt as to his guilt. Less than a week later, Tarwill was shot in the head from a passing coach as he left his club."

Again I believe that both men were aware of my disapproval, given that I had identified the circumstances correctly. During our association, Holmes and I had encountered many instances where the accused would have justifiably served a long prison sentence or been hanged, were it not for the convincing and insistent manner of a competent defence lawyer. I could not reconcile this with my faith in British justice, but I could think of no way that it would ever change.

"Next," Lestrade continued, 'there was Thomas Leroy, last November. He was a small-time thief and well-known to us at the Yard. Inspector Gregson and myself suspected him of murdering a merchant in the Old Kent Road but again, he was acquitted on the testimony of four witnesses. I knew them all, and would have bet my right arm that they were lying but nevertheless, Leroy would be walking the streets of London today had not our killer put a bullet in his skull eight days afterwards."

"You are satisfied," Holmes enquired again, "that these killings were carried out by the same perpetrator?"

"There can be no doubt of it, Mr Holmes. We have ascertained that the weapon that killed Tarwill, Leroy and others that I have yet to mention to you, is one and the same. In February of this year two prisoners who had their capital sentences commuted to long prison terms were finally released, now quite elderly of course and their crimes long forgotten by the public. Donald Rearden was shot like the others and Grace Lightwell was found strangled, both within a fortnight of regaining their freedom. Nor is that the end of this. May saw the shooting, as he walked home from an evening in an ale-house, of Roger Carvell, recently released from Newgate after it was discovered that he was dying from consumption. The prison governor tells me that he believes in Carvell's innocence, and he interceded on his behalf. It was before my time but I've reviewed the case and found it to be fragile at best. Carvell was a mild and inoffensive man who served his time as a model prisoner, but within a month of leaving prison he was dead. It caused no great sensation, and hardly justified a mention on the back page of the newspapers. As far as I know that is the extent of this murderer's work, but I would not be surprised if we heard more of him."

"Are there any further long-standing prisoners due for release?" I asked.

"I've checked on that, Doctor. The next are not due till the coming new year."

"If our man, assuming a man is responsible for these killings, conforms to his present pattern, we have at least two months to work towards his apprehension," Holmes observed. "Have you anything that might be of assistance to us, Lestrade, should we undertake this case?"

The little detective nodded, his bulldog-like face expressing a mixture of relief and gratitude. He plunged a hand deep into his pocket to produce a crumpled piece of paper. "This is evidence you understand, gentlemen. After Mr Holmes has examined it, I must return it to the official files."

Holmes nodded and took up his lens, and I rose to peer over his shoulder. In a cultured script, written on the grimy sheet were the words: *The law will triumph.* It was signed *The Justice Master.*

"The paper, despite its condition, is an expensive one," my friend observed. "Costing, I should think, no less than eight pence a packet. The ink also is of good quality, since it has not smudged or been excessively absorbed. The pen has a new nib and the writing is of one who is quite used to his role as a scribe, possibly because his profession demands it. The strokes suggest the aggressive penmanship of a man, who is almost certainly left-handed. The text implies, as does his choice of victim, that our killer is obsessed with those he sees as escaping justice, and with punishing them personally." He paused, thoughtfully. "Very well, Lestrade, I will look into this, but you need not have hurried from your bed at quite such a pace to get here today."

The inspector regarded Holmes curiously. "Thank you, sir. But how can you tell that I made my way here immediately from rising?"

"It is simplicity itself," Holmes said as he had many times before. "To begin with, the carriage in which you arrived was driven at extraordinary speed, as I heard before you alighted. Also you had run to procure it, since you displayed signs of breathlessness when you entered this room."

Lestrade acknowledged this. "All very true, Mr Holmes, but none of this explains how you deduced that I came here directly."

"Quite so, but the remnant of dried shaving soap behind your left ear points to that."

"Well, I never," the inspector used a handkerchief to wipe his face.

"So, have you anything more to tell us?" Holmes asked.

Our visitor looked a little sheepish, as he answered. "Only that, because of circumstances surrounding this case, I was obliged to mention my asking for your assistance to various individuals. These include some of my superiors at the Yard, and certain members of the legal profession and the courts."

An amused expression spread across Holmes' hawk-like features. "Then I sincerely hope, inspector, that I shall have something enlightening for you to report to them, before long."

"But where will you begin, Holmes?" I enquired.

"In a situation such as this, where our unknown adversary has committed crimes over a period of time, it is advisable to work backwards since more evidence is likely to remain from recent activity. I will therefore concentrate my initial enquiries on the last victim to date. I believe you said that was a Mr Roger Carvell, who was killed in May. Is that not so, Lestrade?"

"That is correct, Mr Holmes."

"And are there any relatives of Mr Carvell?"

"He leaves only a younger brother, Godfrey, as far as I know."

"Excellent!" Holmes rose from his chair and we did likewise. "Pray leave his address, if you have it, with Doctor Watson. I will begin my investigation immediately. Doubtlessly I shall have something to report soon. If there is nothing more that is pertinent, Lestrade, we will bid you good day."

Chapter 2 – Mr Latimer Causes Delay

We gazed from our window as Lestrade's hansom sped out of sight.

"We are leaving, I suppose," I said as I turned and crossed the room to the coat-stand.

"I was not certain that you would consent to accompany me."

"My dear fellow," I began, "I have already explained, in the course of our previous conversation, that the eager young *locum* who is at present managing my practice has assured me that my presence is unnecessary during his tenure. My first thought was to reprimand him for his impudence, but on reflection the situation has provided me with a much-needed respite. Tell me, Holmes, how else would I spend such unoccupied time, if not in accompanying you?"

He regarded me with something approaching sentiment. "Thank you, Watson. I knew I could count on you, as ever."

Having put on our hats and coats, he shouted to Mrs Hudson that we were unlikely to be in for luncheon as we descended the stairs. As we stepped into Baker Street, Holmes raised his arm to summon a passing hansom, only to lower it immediately as it became apparent that an approaching man intended to accost us.

"From the legal profession, I would think."

I glanced at my friend, able for once to match his conclusion. "The sombre apparel and wing collar suggested this to you. That heavy briefcase is probably full of the details of some case or other."

"Your first observation is sound, but the second is not conclusive," he replied as the fellow drew nearer.

"Mr Sherlock Holmes and Doctor Watson, without a doubt." The voice of the man who addressed us was uncommonly deep. It struck me that his narrow features were as hawk-like as those of Holmes, and he stood as high. Although his smile appeared friendly, it did not escape me that his eyes were cold.

"Your presumption is correct, sir," Holmes said. "How can we assist you?"

"My name is David Grantly-Knight, and I am a solicitor, currently attached to the Old Bailey."

When we had shaken hands, he continued : "I am aware, gentlemen, of the case that you are currently engaged upon."

I was momentarily taken aback by this although Holmes was unperturbed, until I recalled that Lestrade had mentioned that certain others were privy to the situation.

"Indeed?" said Holmes.

Mr Grantly-Knight nodded. "Inspector Lestrade has, I believe, acquainted you with certain details of a series of unsolved crimes. I will not detain you, for I merely wish to assure you that I will be glad to furnish any aid you may require in connection with this, and also that my records are available to you."

"That is most thoughtful of you," Holmes acknowledged. "Is there anything in particular that you have to tell us?"

"I have had some involvement already with the circumstances surrounding this affair. On two occasions I have interviewed Mr Henry Latimer, whose profession is reporting the news for *The Daily Clarion.* Throughout our conversations I formed the impression that he had gained knowledge that he was reluctant to share, perhaps something which could suggest the identity of this killer. It was my clerk, Mr Withers, who voiced the opinion that it is likely that you may have greater success than ourselves, hence my approach to you today."

"Our thanks to you, sir. You may be certain that we will consult you, should the need arise. It would be prudent, I think, for us to divert from our intended destination and seek out Mr Latimer now."

"Here are his whereabouts, Mr Holmes." He passed a page from a notebook to my friend.

"I assume that, should we need to, a telegram to the courts will find you," I ventured.

"It will, without fail," said the lawyer. "Scotland Yard is not alone in its concern for the apprehension of this murderer. I would be appreciative of a report of your progress, from time to time."

Holmes nodded, I thought without enthusiasm. "When there is anything to report, we will do so promptly, of course."

"Excellent." Mr Grantly-Knight consulted his pocket-watch. "But I see that I am due in court, very shortly. Good day to you both. I look forward to hearing from you."

With a farewell gesture, he strode away abruptly.

Holmes watched their departure for a moment, before turning to me.

"What do you make of him, Watson?"

"He seems as anxious to see this man caught, as was Inspector Lestrade."

"Oh, he is, and that Mr Grantly-Knight intends to use the resulting successful prosecution to place himself in a position to put on judge's robes, I am quite certain. If ever I saw ambition consuming a man, it is in him. However, the suggestion of an interview with Mr Henry Latimer is sound, and can probably be concluded before luncheon. Ah, I see that a hansom is approaching at a slow pace, which probably means that it has discharged its fare. Be so good as to hail it, while I ascertain our destination from Mr Grantly-Knight's note."

"Queen's Consort Street, Parson's Green, Fulham!" My friend shouted to the driver as we entered the cab. The man acknowledged at once and whipped up the horse, sending several urchins scurrying out of our path.

"Some of your Irregulars, Holmes?" I asked as we passed.

He shook his head and said nothing, remaining in silent thought until we reached a street of small but well-kept houses where the hansom was brought to rest.

"Not a careful man, I think, judging by the state of his front garden."

We strode along a short path with overgrown foliage to either side. Holmes rapped on the door with his cane, and it swung open almost at once, to reveal a middle-aged man of medium height who reminded me instantly of a ferret. His wary eyes were set in a thin face and the set of his mouth was unfriendly.

"What can I do for you gentlemen?" he said without a change of expression.

"We would be grateful," replied my friend, "if you could spare us a little of your time to talk of certain recent crimes with which I understand you have spent some time in acquainting yourself."

"I will tell the law nothing," he said emphatically. "They are quite able to do their own chasing. Heaven knows they have done nothing to help me."

Holmes nodded. "So I have heard, but we are not the law. My name is Sherlock Holmes, and I am a private consulting detective. The gentleman who accompanies me is my friend and colleague, Doctor John Watson. May we enter and discuss the matter?"

Mr Latimer stared at us for a moment. "Not the law, you say?"

"I have helped Scotland Yard now and then, but there have been times when they have proved to be an obstacle."

"Never more so, I have found, than when one is trying to get at the truth." He opened the door wider and stood back. "Very well. Come in gentlemen."

We were led to a large room which Mr Latimer apparently used as a study. Three desks were piled with papers, and files had been stacked untidily along a number of shelves. In a corner, past issues of *The Daily Clarion* adorned an upright chair. Pale light streamed through the single window enabling me to see him more clearly, and I saw in his face the signs of years of strain.

"Please be seated." He indicated two rather worn armchairs which we found to be quite comfortable, before offering us whisky which we both declined.

"We were directed here," Holmes began, "by Mr David Grantly-Knight, a solicitor with chambers at the Old Bailey."

"I know the man. He shares my interest in bringing this killer to justice."

"You have perceived, of course, the link between the victims?"

"I have. It became obvious, as soon as I compared their situations by an examination of the files at *The Clarion*. What do you think, Mr Holmes? What makes a man pursue people who have killed others and got away with it? Do you think he sees himself as God?"

My friend nodded slowly. "That is a possibility that I have yet to confirm or deny. It may be that he has an abnormally strong sense of justice and seeks to correct what he sees as the shortcomings of the law. Have you, Mr Latimer, any idea as to the identity of our killer? I understand that your investigation on behalf of your employer was relentless."

Mr Latimer sat back in his chair with a thoughtful expression. I could see that he was considering something, possibly whether he should divulge information that he had hitherto withheld.

"Gentlemen, I must confess that I have not been entirely honest with you," he said then.

"How so, sir?" I responded, while Holmes remained silent and still.

"When you arrived I feigned ignorance as to your reputations and purpose, because I am weary of the treatment I receive from the official force and others. The truth is that, as a reporter working for one of our leading newspapers, I am very much aware of both. Does that surprise you, Mr Holmes?"

A faint smile crossed my friend's face. "Not at all. You would be a very obtuse investigator indeed, if you had not heard of some of the outrages and scandals that I have been fortunate enough to be of assistance to Scotland Yard in resolving. If you were so informed, then you would have been confronted by a mention of my involvement from time to time."

"As indeed I was, many times. Tell me, sir, in the course of your profession, have you encountered Mr Berkeley Croft?"

I shook my head.

"I recall the name from my index," Holmes responded. "Like yourself, Mr Latimer, he has written articles for *The Clarion.*"

"But no more, regretfully, for Croft knew his job well. Nevertheless he was foolish enough, some little time ago, to become involved in – shall we say - a slight indiscretion. I will not go into the nature of it, but the editor of *The Clarion* was concerned that a possible scandal might smear the paper's name and Croft was dismissed."

"Was he also concerned in your investigation of these murders?" Holmes enquired.

"Not up until then. As an old friend, I have met him several times since. We were enjoying a drink together in a tavern much frequented by those of our calling when he confided in me that he had maintained his communications with most of the network of informants that he had built up over the years, reporting is in his blood he told me, and that one of these had not only accidentally caught the killer in the act, but had recognised him."

"Have you not informed the official force of this?" I asked.

"Clearly I could not, since I have yet to meet Croft again to ascertain whether he has managed to persuade his source, or to offer him a sufficient sum, to divulge the identity of the killer. Also, as I have said, the officers of the Yard have refused to aid my investigations in the past."

I was about to retort that it was Mr Latimer's duty to inform the authorities of his discoveries, when Holmes silenced me with a movement of his hand.

"Have you arranged such a meeting?" He asked Mr Latimer.

"I have, for tomorrow night. However, I am sure that you, gentlemen, will appreciate my position, when I tell you that I am not prepared to reveal the time or where it is to be. If you would be good enough to call here the following day, however, I will have had sufficient time to prepare my submission to my employer and I will identify the killer for you. If you then wish to use this to continue your endeavours, or to inform the law, you may do so as you wish."

"You wish us to call here? Not at the offices of *The Clarion?*"

The reporter shook his head. "I am rarely to be found there. My position necessitates that I circulate between various sites that are, or are likely to be, of interest to my readers." He rose from his chair. "Until then, gentlemen."

We arrived back at our lodgings in time for luncheon. After enjoying Mrs Hudson's chicken pie followed by fresh raspberries and cream, none of which held much interest for Holmes, we settled into our armchairs.

"I perceive that you are restless, Watson," my friend said from behind his newspaper. "You are constantly shifting your position and you have not turned a page of your book for at least five minutes."

"I am at a loss to understand, Holmes, why we are sitting here after consuming that excellent luncheon."

He lowered his paper and I saw an amused twinkle in his eyes. "Where then, would you have us be?"

"I had expected that we would be continuing our investigation. Although we are not meeting Mr Latimer until the day after tomorrow, we could be interviewing Mr Godfrey Carvell, the brother of the killer's last victim."

"That had occurred to me, but I decided that our present line of enquiry is most likely to advance our investigation. We can, after all, revert to seeking out Mr Carvell should it prove to be necessary. As for Mr Latimer, it is by no means certain that it will be so long before we encounter him again."

At that, he would say no more. We continued to read until dinner was served, after which Holmes took up his violin and played a long and mournful tune which he proudly announced to be of his own composition. This had the effect of causing a lowering of my spirit, and it was still quite early when I bade him goodnight and retired. I slept well and awoke before seven. When Mrs Hudson had brought hot water, I washed and shaved and emerged from my room for breakfast. To my surprise, since he was not usually an early riser, Holmes was already at the table.

"As usual, Watson, the kippers are excellent. Allow me to call Mrs Hudson to serve you some."

"I would be most grateful."

He did so and we enjoyed them together, in companionable silence until we were drinking our second cup of coffee.

"Well, Holmes, how do you propose we occupy our time today? Have you anything else on hand, while we await word from Mr Latimer?"

He replaced his empty cup. "Doubtlessly you were about to suggest that we take some exercise, since it is a fine morning, but I have many additions to make to my index. However, I should have completed them by the time Mrs Hudson serves our luncheon, and a stroll around Hyde Park or St James's would be welcome then."

"I trust it will not disturb you if I remain here and review my notes of the past week?"

"Not at all, old fellow. My task requires little concentration."

And so we spent the morning. Throughout this time I sensed that Holmes was in a state of expectancy, awaiting some news or event which would propel us into immediate action. Nothing transpired, and I laid aside the last of my papers almost at the same moment that our landlady appeared. Facing him across the table I sensed a mounting tension like that of a coiled spring, but he said nothing. I knew this mood of old, its cause was enforced inactivity which was abhorrent to him.

"Holmes," I began when our meal was over and his intensity had become intolerable, "am I correct in surmising that you intend to visit Mr Latimer before he expects us? You remarked as much, yesterday."

"Your observations do you credit, doctor, although they are not based on firm facts. You are, however, quite correct in…."

He halted in mid-sentence, interrupted by the loud peals of the door-bell. Moments later, Mrs Hudson showed in a short, stout man, much flustered and nervously holding his hat against his stomach.

"Mr Joshua Pine, to see Mr Holmes," she announced and immediately withdrew.

Our visitor looked at Holmes, then at me, then back to my friend. "Mr Holmes? Mr Sherlock Holmes?" he gasped.

"It is I that you seek," Holmes informed him quietly. "Pray calm yourself and let us be seated. The basket chair, I think you will find, is comfortable."

"Thank you, sirs," Mr Pine said when we were settled. "No, I will not take brandy, for I am anxious to secure your advice regarding an experience that has shaken me to my bones. I am in mortal terror!"

Both Holmes and I leaned forward in our chairs so that we might give our full attention, and I was surprised to see an expression of amusement pass quickly across my friend's countenance.

"Take a moment to compose yourself, and then relate to us the circumstances that have given you such a fright," Holmes advised. "Then we may seek a remedy or solution."

"Yes, yes, that would be most desirable." Sweat ran down Mr Pine's reddened face, as he struggled to control his agitation.

"Begin when you are ready, then."

Our visitor shifted in his chair. "I have recently moved into a very old house in Hammersmith. No sooner had I gathered my possessions around me than several residents of the neighbouring dwellings began to call upon me, all with the same gruesome tale. Apparently the premises were occupied, nearly a century ago, by a lascar. He was a violent man, his temper easily aroused, and one day he took an axe to two women who had done nothing more offensive than call upon him in the hope of a donation for a religious charity. I found this story interesting, of course, but I was horrified when I learned that this drama had been seen to be carried out time after time by successive tenants of the house I now live in. I thought no more of this for a week or two, but last night I saw the spectacle with my own eyes. It was horrible, I tell you, and the spectre assaulted me!"

He turned towards us, revealing a bloody gash along his jawbone.

"I was most fortunate to escape I ran from the house as if the devil pursued me, because I felt that he did."

I held my pencil poised over my notebook in the short silence that fell upon the room. Through our half-open window, the clatter of horses' hooves and the distant calls of various tradesmen came to us faintly.

"Most curious," Holmes observed then. "When you saw the lascar attack the women, did they appear solid? In other words, were they flesh and blood such as are you and I?"

"No, not a bit like that. They were like smoke drifting and taking shape and then drifting again."

"And yet one of them was able to inflict a solid blow upon you."

"But," Mr Pine stammered, "that is the way of ghosts, is it not? We know not if they are solid or have the consistency of mist or fog."

"Perhaps, but I have yet to encounter such an occurrence that cannot be explained logically. Tell me, Mr Pine, what would you have me do to exorcise this most vicious trespasser from the supposed hereafter? Are you certain that a priest would not have suited you better?"

Our visitor passed a hand across his damp brow, his disquiet evident. "Well, I am much relieved that you do not entertain such notions of the supernatural, Mr Holmes. May I suggest therefore, that you come with me now to Hammersmith to see for yourself any trace that this imposter has left? If he is mortal, he will have left some sign of his presence, surely?"

Holmes nodded slowly. "Undoubtedly, but I fear that I am unable to attend immediately." He glanced at his pocket-watch. "However, I can assure you that I will be taking certain actions to remedy this situation later today." He rose abruptly.

"And now, Mr Pine, we will bid you good-day, as Watson and I have much to discuss before any steps can be taken."

Mr Pine struggled to his feet. "Well, Mr Holmes, I am sure that you know best how to set about this. I must go to my employment now, but I am sure I will see some results from your attention soon."

"Indeed, you will," Holmes assured him with a twinkle in his eye.

After a quick gesture of farewell our visitor was gone, and to my absolute surprise Holmes sat down heavily and shook with laughter.

Chapter 3 – The Unexpected Victim

The hurried footsteps descending our stairs ceased, and the door slammed. I gazed upon my friend in disbelief.

"My dear Holmes, it is most unlike you to take a humorous view of a client's difficulties. That man was beside himself with fear."

"Indeed he was," he produced a handkerchief and wiped tears from his eyes, "but the fear was that we should become aware of his deception, and was the only genuine aspect of his presence."

"Your reasoning escapes me."

"Had you recognised him, as I did, you also would have had your suspicions at once. His true name is Norbert Crowe, as you would discover were you to read the posters advertising the productions of little-known plays in some of our back-street theatres."

"The man is an actor?"

"Indeed, and has been for many years, before falling on hard times recently."

"But there must be some substance to his story."

"About a ghost? You are aware of my conclusions on all matters supernatural."

I shook my head. "No, I was thinking of the wound to his face."

"Theatrical make-up, applied rather excessively." Holmes looked as if he might dissolve into mirth again, at the memory of our client's attempt to deceive him. "Did you not notice the traces of it remaining on his fingertips?"

"I confess that I did not, but what could have been the true purpose of his visit?"

My friend got to his feet. "I believe he was hired and sent to delay us with this nonsense."

"Do you mean – ah, I have it – our intended early visit to Mr Latimer?"

"Precisely. Mr Latimer was adamant in his intention to conceal from us the time and place of his meeting with his ex-colleague, Mr Berkeley Croft. I proposed to arrive near his house in a hansom, and follow Mr Latimer. I wished to interview Mr Croft myself, but clearly I was anticipated."

"Mr Latimer is a wily man to deal with, evidently."

"He is, after all, a reporter for a newspaper. The fault here, however, is my own. I should have expected him to take some sort of precaution to prevent our interference." He picked up his hat and cane. "It may be that it is not yet too late. We may yet find him still at home if we depart now. Come, Watson, I will hail a cab while you inform Mrs Hudson that we will not be in for dinner."

I did as my friend requested, but reluctantly, for the cooking smells emanating from below were causing my awareness of my growing appetite to increase. The resignation in our landlady's reply held no surprise for me, for she was long accustomed to Holmes' irregular and peculiar habits.

After a short conversation, the cab driver agreed that we should retain his services for as much of the evening as required. The streets were quieter than is usual for the time of day, and we were in Fulham before long. Except for minimal remarks in answer to my observations of the passing parade of people and localities, Holmes remained silent during the journey. I came to realise that his concern was for more than the lateness of our repeated visit to Mr Latimer's premises, and concluded that the reporter's safety might be in question also.

The hansom was brought to a halt in Queen's Consort Street, under a huge oak that would partially conceal it were Mr Latimer to look from his window. The light was fading rapidly now, and the windows of the adjacent houses became illuminated one by one. Holmes' gaze was fixed intently on Mr Latimer's home, but the curtains were not drawn. Neither did we see the flicker of a flame as a lamp was lit.

"It is as I feared, Watson," Holmes said in a tone of disgust, "We arrived too late."

He sprang from the carriage and crossed the street at a run, hammering on Mr Latimer's door as he reached it. There was no response, and after pressing his nose to the window pane, my friend shook his head in exasperation and returned to the hansom.

"Mr Latimer's use of Joshua Pine to delay our pursuit was apparently successful. He anticipated us well."

"How do we proceed now?" I asked as he resumed his seat.

I was never to receive a reply, for at that moment a police coach swept past us and halted almost opposite. We watched as a man alighted and strode urgently to Mr Latimer's house.

After a moment we left the hansom and made to join him.

"Good evening, Lestrade," Holmes called.

The inspector had been about to knock on the door. "Mr Holmes! I had not expected to find you here."

"But I am not surprised to encounter you. Unless I am in error, you are attempting to inform Mr Latimer's relatives of his death."

"How on earth did you know?"

"I cannot perceive of any other reason why you should arrive in such haste. Dr Watson and myself have interviewed Mr Latimer previously, and learned that he was to meet someone of significance, this evening. He thought it probable that he would discover the identity of the killer about whom you consulted me, but would not reveal details of the appointment. I therefore determined to follow him, but was unexpectedly delayed. It occurred to me that Mr Latimer's life could have been in jeopardy, had the killer somehow become aware of his intentions. You need not bother with further attempts to attract attention here – Mr Latimer lived alone. If he had any relatives, they live elsewhere."

The little detective nodded sadly. "Would that you had been successful in your pursuit. It may have been that a double murder could have been avoided."

"A *double* murder, did you say?" I have rarely seen such surprise on my friend's face.

"Indeed. Mr Latimer and the man in his company. A Mr Berkeley Croft."

"The former colleague who could have revealed all to us. How were they killed?"

"In the same fashion as this killer's other male victims – a bullet in the head."

"But this time our adversary has broken the pattern, for these were not men who had been convicted."

A faint trace of amusement crossed Lestrade's bulldog-like face, and I sensed his awareness of something that was unknown to us.

"That is not entirely true, Mr Holmes. In fact, had I not met you here, I would have called upon you at Baker Street to inform you of this turn of events. You see, I learned from Mr Grantly-Knight, of the Old Bailey, that he had spoken to you and suggested that you consider Mr Latimer as part of your investigation. I became curious enough to consult our files, and to my astonishment I discovered that Mr Latimer too, was once convicted of a capital crime. The victim was a woman of the streets, and Latimer was released on appeal. I must say that the case against him was far from conclusive."

"So with him our killer continued his pattern, after all. But what of the other man?"

"There our murderer has claimed a victim for no other reason but to silence him, assuming that he was in possession of the information that Mr Latimer sought. There is something else I would share with you." The official detective withdrew two scraps of paper from his pocket. "First this, further evidence that this crime is linked to the others. I found it pinned to Mr Latimer's coat."

Holmes took the crumpled sheet, a half-page torn from a notebook, and I peered over his shoulder to read the scant words.

Truth will not be denied. The guilty will be punished.

The Justice Master.

After a long scrutiny with his lens, he handed it back to the inspector.

"Much the same as the first, I think. Pray show me the other evidence."

The second paper was of a lesser quality than the first, and written in pencilled script.

To Mr Croft,

Be sure to bring the money, and I will tell you.

G.C.

"That was found on the person of the other dead man," Lestrade informed us somewhat unnecessarily.

Holmes put away his lens. "I can deduce little from it, other than that the writer is a person of at least rudimentary education, and is either of a nervous disposition or writes with a damaged hand. He is probably not a man of means, since the paper is not from a notebook but has been ripped from a periodical or some work of literature."

"I can see that the man has some knowledge of English, by his use of punctuation," I acknowledged, "but how did you arrive at the conclusion that he suffers from a nervous ailment or that his hand is damaged?"

"That caused me to wonder, also," Lestrade added.

"It is quite simple," Holmes pointed out. "When someone writes in such a scrawling fashion, and leaves an imprint that can only be the result of pressing a pencil onto the paper with quite unnecessary force, what else am I to conclude but that he is unable to control his hand for either or both of these reasons?"

I nodded, wondering, as I had many times before, why I had not seen this immediately.

Inspector Lestrade mumbled something which could have been, "Of course".

"You have doubtlessly identified the writer already, inspector, for the initials 'G.C.' are those of only one person we know as yet to be connected to this case. I refer, of course, to Mr Godfrey Carvel, the younger brother of the killer's sixth victim."

"Who we were on our way to interview, when we encountered Mr Grantly-Knight in Baker Street," I recalled.

"Precisely. It seems as if this affair has turned full circle, inasmuch as we find ourselves back at our point of outset."

"Well, gentlemen," Lestrade said then, "it seems that there is nothing to be done here. I have made arrangements for the bodies to be taken to the mortuary and the investigation into these murders will now be continued. If you so choose, Mr Holmes, you need trouble no further with this."

"I think I can find the time to look into things a little more deeply," my friend said with a twinkle in his eye. "As it is with the Yard, the Baker Street files are never closed without a satisfactory conclusion."

Shortly after the inspector left, we returned to our waiting hansom. The hour was by now getting late, and on returning to our lodgings we saw that no light showed from Mrs Hudson's quarters. She had, however, been kind enough to leave us a cold supper of meat and pickles which I partook of gratefully, while Holmes repaired immediately to his room after a murmured 'Good night'.

The following morning I sat down to breakfast to discover that he had already gone out. His bacon and eggs he had left almost untouched, although the coffee pot was more than half empty.

When Mrs Hudson brought my own food she looked upon my friend's leavings with disapproval, but made no comment. It was shortly after she withdrew, that I heard his returning footfalls upon the stairs.

"Ah, Watson!" he exclaimed as he entered. "You will be ready, I trust, for an excursion to Tottenham when you have finished eating."

"Tottenham?" I queried.

"The current place of residence of Mr Godfrey Carvell."

I nodded. "Be so good as to allow me a few minutes to drink a second cup of coffee, and I will join you." I reduced the contents of my cup by about half. "Where have you been, Holmes?"

"Something occurred to me as I sat down to breakfast, and it seemed prudent to confirm the notion. I expect the replies to several telegrams, later."

I stood up and reached for my coat. "I am at your disposal, old fellow."

We were fortunate enough to find a hansom delivering a fare, further along Baker Street. During the journey of almost five miles, Holmes sat deep in thought with his head upon his chest. I can recall him speaking but once, in answer to my question regarding his visit to the telegraph office.

"A possible further connection between the victims suggested itself to me, but it may come to nothing."

We arrived at Chestnut Walk, a tiny street poised on the very edge of the village. Beyond the few houses sheep grazed peacefully in fields the extent of which were beyond our view, and the blissful quiet was medicine to the nerves. Holmes requested the cabby to wait, and the man agreed cheerfully before leading his horse across the road to a drinking-trough standing near a small but evidently much-used tavern.

Mr Godfrey Carvell answered his door at the first knock. He was a narrow-faced man, thin-lipped with pince-nez perched upon a beak-like nose. I noticed immediately that two fingers were missing from his right hand, as Holmes had deduced.

"Can I assist you gentlemen?"

"That is most likely, Mr Carvell," my friend replied. "My name is Sherlock Holmes, and this is my friend and colleague, Doctor John Watson. There have been developments regarding the unsolved death of your brother, and Scotland Yard has requested that I assist them with their enquiries. May we come in and speak to you?"

For an instant he stared blankly, before stepping back and opening the door wider. "Very well. Come in, gentlemen."

He led us down a short corridor into a rather sparsely-furnished room. Four mismatched armchairs surrounded an unlit fire and the small bookcase boasted few volumes. The walls were dark and the windows small. It seemed to me a cheerless place.

"Please be seated."

Holmes and I complied, and I was glad to discover that the chairs were more comfortable than they appeared.

"We are chiefly interested," my friend began, "in your association with Mr Berkeley Croft, the former reporter. It has come to our attention that you had obtained some valuable information for him, for which he was prepared to pay."

The poor light reflected darkly upon Mr Carvell's pince-nez, as he lowered himself into a chair and regarded us with a wary smile.

"Mr Croft did indeed pay me handsomely, for a single name. He intended to divulge this to a colleague, who will see that it is published in today's editions. He seemed to think that supplying this information indirectly to *The Clarion* would aid him in regaining his old position there, and explained to me that his colleague had undertaken to emphasise the source of his article to the editor. I very much hope that he did, for Mr Croft struck me as an agreeable fellow."

"I regret to inform you," Holmes said after a moment, "that both Mr Croft and his colleague have been murdered."

Mr Carvell sat very still for a moment, then he wrung his hands in despair. "Oh, good heavens, I told him to be careful. You really cannot speak of people like that indiscriminately. They find out, and they are dangerous."

"Indeed so," I said. "It is as well that the killer seems to be unaware that it was you who confided his name to Mr Croft, otherwise it is conceivable that he might attempt to silence you also."

I saw an amused smile flit across Holmes' face and instantly disappear. He had discerned, as I had known he would, my tactic in inducing our host to speak to us with frankness.

"Yes, I do see that." Mr Carvell had paled visibly.

"It would be best then," Holmes suggested, "if you were to tell us all that you know. The sooner that this murderer is apprehended, the safer the streets of London will be."

"Well, if Mr Croft is no longer with us, I imagine that it no longer matters to him. I will tell you exactly the facts as I related them to him, and then you must judge for yourself what must be done." He spent a moment, collecting his thoughts. "Some time before Roger was killed – this past February, I think it was – I was returning home from an evening attending one of the new music hall productions, when I chanced to take a short cut through Brasshouse Street, in Soho. There I saw a man bending over a woman who lay senseless on the pavement, and I realised that he was in the act of removing a piece of rope or twine from around her neck. My first thought was to retrace my steps, but it was too late. He had seen me."

"You arrived there immediately after the murder of Miss Grace Lightwell," Holmes confirmed. "You may consider yourself fortunate, Mr Carvell, that you lived to tell the tale."

"Yes," he swallowed noisily, and I noticed that his hands were clenched into fists. "Especially as he recognised me. I have seen him once or twice in the local taverns of that area, and have heard him referred to in conversation as Vernon Stark, although I suspect that not to be his real name."

"Pray explain how you reached that conclusion."

"On a previous occasion I had seen him approached by a gentleman who seemed to know him as someone else, but Stark denied ever having met the fellow before. The man left the bar shaking his head, much confused."

Holmes nodded. "Continue please, with your narrative."

"When he had left the body of that poor woman he approached me and said that if I ever spoke of what I had seen to anyone, he would find me and kill me in the most painful way imaginable. You should have seen him, Mr Holmes, he was very convincing."

"I do not doubt that. Pray describe him for us, to the best of your recollection."

"He is not a tall man, he has a red birthmark high on his forehead and the smile of a madman. That is all I can tell you."

"Not quite, I think. After Stark threatened you with such consequences, why did you confide in Mr Croft?"

"Look around you, gentlemen," Mr Carvell sighed. "I am not a rich man, barely able to pay my rent and feed myself.

When Mr Croft offered me so much money for so little, I was tempted and decided to take the risk."

"But this was the killer of your brother also, a few months later," I reminded him.

"I was not certain of that. In any case, my disclosure could well have led to his arrest. I should perhaps make it clear that, although I was of course upset by Roger's death, his almost total absence from my life had long caused me to think of him as lost to me. Consequently, the shock of his demise so soon after his release was not as severe as it otherwise might have been."

Holmes was silent for what seemed a long time, although Mr Carvell showed no signs of impatience.

"Are you quite sure that you have now told us everything?" Holmes raised his head from his apparent examination of the threadbare carpet. "Sometimes it is details, no matter how small, that cast a great deal of light on things that previously appeared to be unfathomable."

A thought struck me then. "You did, I would think, visit your brother in prison?"

"From time to time. He was often reluctant to see me, expressing the wish that I should be getting on with my life in more pleasant surroundings."

"And there is nothing that passed between you during those visits that could be significant to our investigation?"

Mr Carvell shook his head slowly. "I can think of nothing more." Then, as Holmes and I were getting to our feet: "Wait! There was a single instance, but I can see no relevance."

"Possibly we may be able to glean something from it," Holmes said hopefully. "Kindly relate it, to the best of your recollection."

"During my visits to Newgate, Roger and I talked mostly of the past. We spoke of better times when we were young and the world was to us a wonderful place. I was his only connection to his former life. One day he told me, to my surprise, of a single unexpected visit from a woman. He had thought at first that she represented one of those well-meaning groups whose mission in life is to reform those who have been convicted, or a religious group that seeks to encourage remorse, but by the time she left he was unsure of her purpose. He reflected later that almost all her questions sprang from his supposed crime, rather than to ascertain whether he harboured any regret. He gained the impression that she had sought to confirm his guilt and, despite the insistence of his innocence that he had maintained from the first, believed that she had done so."

"Can you recall how long ago this transpired?"

"I would say shortly before his release."

"Did your brother describe this woman?"

"He did indeed. As I remember, he said she was tall, dark-haired and quite beautiful. What struck him most, however, was her bitterness. He could not say why it should be, but he remarked that she must have acid in her veins."

"Extraordinary," but I saw from Holmes expression that something had rung true with him. "She left no name, of course?"

"Strangely, she did. She introduced herself as Lilly. Also, it has just come to me that Roger mentioned that she made some vague reference to murder, stating the opinion that it should, without appeal or consideration of circumstance, result in a meeting of the perpetrator with the hangman."

Chapter 4 – The Buccaneer

I pushed away my plate. Mrs Hudson's fish pie never varied in its excellence.

"What have you learned, Holmes?"

My friend has forsaken his half-eaten luncheon, as several telegrams arrived. As he tore the envelopes open, one by one, his expression became one of satisfaction.

"I had surmised a connection between the victims, before we visited Mr Carvell. Now it is confirmed."

"I confess to believing that we had covered all aspects of the victims' similarities, in our previous discussions."

He sat more upright in his chair. "For a while, Watson, I, too, could imagine no unexplored path regarding the murders. Then it came to me that the victims might have been visited, during their long terms of imprisonment, by the same person or persons. I therefore despatched telegrams to the governors of the prisons concerned, and their answers bear out my supposition."

"The woman who called herself 'Lilly', that Mr Carvell was told about by his brother?" I ventured.

"Indeed. The prison records bear this out. Her full name is Lilly Bastock, according to the signatures in the prison registers."

"Can it be that she is behind these crimes? I cannot believe that a woman can be the 'Justice Master.'

"As always, you allow yourself to be swayed by a pretty face," Holmes said with some amusement. "That could conceivably be a fatal error. It is certainly unlikely in this instance, I concede, bearing in mind the experience of Mr Carvell and the nature of the crimes, but far from impossible if there is more than one killer. You will recall that we have encountered such capable women before now, which proves that on occasion they are far from the weaker sex, the helpless creatures as many are inclined to believe. However, as things are at present it is far more likely that she is involved in a different way, such as in gathering facts about the intended victims to aid the murderer in his quest. Doubtlessly our investigation will reveal more as we progress."

Both Holmes and I had declined dessert. Unusual, as he did not fail to remark, as that was for me, it was a common feature of his eating habits. There was, I realised as I lifted it, more coffee in the pot, and we had scarcely drained our cups for the second time when the loud peals of the door-bell interrupted our conversation.

"Mr Grantly-Knight has paid us a visit, I think," he murmured after a moment.

"How can you know that?"

"There is no mystery, Watson," he smiled. "I simply heard him speak to Mrs Hudson when she answered the summons to the door. You will observe that the window is partly open and recall that he has an unusually distinctive voice."

We heard quick footfalls upon the stairs, and the slower sounds of our landlady in his wake, before the door swung open. Mrs Hudson hardly had time to announce our visitor before he entered. There was an eagerness about him that

Holmes had remarked upon before, and it did not appear to have diminished.

"Gentlemen," he began, "I must apologise for descending upon you without an appointment. I encountered Inspector Lestrade earlier, and he reported that Mr Latimer, to whom I directed you has become the killer's latest victim."

"That is debatable," Holmes answered. "Would you care to sit, Mr Grantly-Knight?"

"Thank you no, for I have little time. I was passing near Baker Street and thought to enquire after your progress. Is Mr Latimer's death in question, then?"

"Not at all. I meant that it is unknown as to who is the latest victim, Mr Latimer or Mr Croft."

A frown crossed his hawkish face. "Ah, of course. Mr Latimer's ex-colleague."

"Quite so."

"Lestrade mentioned also that you intend to call upon the younger Mr Carvell."

"That enquiry was concluded before luncheon."

Our visitor's face lit up with expectation. "Did anything new transpire?"

"Only that several victims were visited during their confinement by the same woman."

"Is she known to us?"

"The name she signed in the prison registers was 'Lilly Bastock'."

"I can recall no previous proceedings involving anyone of that name," Mr Grantly-Knight concluded after a moment of consideration. "Possibly she was from one of those organisations that seek to reform criminals. I see no connection to our murderer."

His expression became one of disappointment. Consulting his pocket-watch, he made to announce his departure, but Holmes spoke first.

"Nevertheless, I would be obliged if you would advise Inspector Lestrade of our discovery that this women could be involved, should you encounter him again before we do. Good day to you, sir."

A hurried reply, and Mr Grantly-Knight was gone from our sight.

"You resent that man, Holmes. It is obvious to me, because I know you. Is it his manner, which seems to suggest that he is employing us, or his determination to use us for his own advancement?"

My friend scowled. "Both, doubtlessly. He said he happened to be passing near Baker Street. Pah!"

We repaired to our usual armchairs. "I presume that we would advance our enquiries if we could find this woman. Is that your view, Holmes?"

"That it will probably aid us, yes, but there is something else that I have realised from these telegrams."

"I see nothing more."

"It is the dates of her visits that are significant. Each took place *after it became known that the prisoner was soon to be released.* Again, this suggests some sort of crusade against those that the Justice Master strongly believes should have been hanged for their crimes."

"So how do we proceed?"

"Clearly, we must find this woman."

"Your index can assist us, perhaps?"

Holmes shook head thoughtfully. "The description is not definitive enough. It could point to several rather unsavoury women that I could bring to mind."

"Scotland Yard, then?"

"It seems we have little alternative, although I am always reluctant to enlist the help of the official force, as you know." He stood up, hurriedly. "Nevertheless, what must be, must be. Come Watson, let us see if Lestrade will allow us to inspect their files."

We put on our hats and coats and went out, feeling the chill autumn wind. There were no hansoms in evidence, but we had walked no further than twenty yards when a carriage pulled by a frisky grey horse overtook us to deliver its fare ahead. We quickened our pace to board it, and were soon on our way.

"Have you any suspicions as to who this woman might be?" I asked him again when we had left Baker Street behind.

"Several possibilities have occurred to me but, as I have indicated, I cannot yet be sure. If we are unsuccessful in gaining access to the Records Room at the yard, our remaining recourses are a thorough scrutiny of my index or to depend on the efficiency of the Irregulars, but I hold out no great hope that these will prove to be of assistance. There is simply not enough data."

I reflected upon how sparse Mr Carvell's description was. When we arrived at the Yard, we were informed by the Desk Sergeant that Inspector Lestrade was not in the building. My heart sank, for I was well aware of the effect on Holmes' disposition when the progress of a case was halted by minor obstacles, but next moment all was well as Inspector Gregson appeared in a doorway.

"Mr Holmes and Doctor Watson! Good afternoon, gentlemen. What brings you here?" He inclined his flaxen head suspiciously. "You are not seeking to put the official force in a bad light, I hope. The newspapers have been severely critical lately."

"You seem in a jovial mood, Gregson," said Holmes. "I perceive that you have gained some recognition."

The Inspector looked back over his shoulder. "You mean because of the office I emerged from? Well, yes, there has been some rearrangement."

"As to your remark, I can assure you that our present investigation will in no way damage the reputation of the Yard. It was, in fact, Inspector Lestrade who suggested it at the outset."

"Lestrade, I believe, is pursuing an enquiry."

"So I have been informed. Can we, therefore, request your assistance?"

"Perhaps. What is it that you require?"

Holmes gestured towards the corridor near the corner of the room. "An hour in your Records Room, if that is permissible."

"Inspector Gregson! I have your man!" The cry came from a young constable who had just entered the building with a surly ruffian in his grip. Gregson's expression deepened, indicating to Holmes and myself that the intrusion was of a serious nature.

"I am aware, Mr Holmes, that Inspector Lestrade has permitted this before, although of course it is highly irregular. And I recall, that on at least one occasion, that I have accompanied you in the Records Room myself in the course of an official investigation. Currently, I am in the midst of a case against a dangerous criminal gang. Therefore, if you gentlemen would care to proceed alone and inform the officer on duty that I have granted you access…" He gestured in the direction of the corridor. "I am sure that you will remember the way."

We strode along a dull corridor, and presently I sat across a table from Holmes in the musty room. Several times he withdrew heavy ledgers from the shelves, sometimes making notes and sometimes returning the volumes without interest or comment.

"Allow me to assist you," I suggested.

"Thank you, Watson, but I fear that you would not recognise what we are seeking."

I felt rather put out at this, but of course he was right. Holmes' knowledge of London criminals was of a depth that I could not hope to approach.

In the silence that followed I could hear the occasional heavy tread in the corridor outside. The smell of stale cigar or pipe smoke hung heavily in here, and there was no window to open. Not for the first time I let my eyes wander along the surrounding walls, across the laden shelves that contained accounts of so many who had flouted the law and caused loss or misery to the people of our capital.

I returned my glance to my friend, realising that I had been daydreaming for longer than I had thought, to find him writing furiously. When he had finished he favoured me with a triumphant smile.

"There were three possibilities, Watson, but one of these was killed by her husband – hardly a love match – and another is presently residing in Holloway. The remaining woman fits Mr Carvell's description well, and has a colourful history. We can be fairly certain that it is she whom we seek."

"Who is she, Holmes?"

"She fits the description we have of Lilly Bastock. She has spent her life in various professions on the streets of London. Her parentage is unknown, but it is thought she had at least one sibling. After spending part of her early years as a beggar, and then a pickpocket, she became a lady of the night for a time, and then married one Jethro Porter, now deceased. On her husband's death she assumed ownership of a dockside tavern, which she still runs."

"Is there any indication of her connection to the victims of the Justice Master, or to prisons?"

"None that is recorded here, which is why we will take some ale in her establishment this evening."

Our journey back to Baker Street was conducted in silence, as I had expected. I knew my friend well enough to do him the courtesy of not attempting to converse, for he was preoccupied with the various possibilities suggested by the woman's involvement in this affair.

As we regained our sitting-room I consulted my pocket-watch, and was amazed to discover that dinner-time was almost upon us. Holmes also had realised this, for instead of settling himself in an armchair he went directly to sit at the table. As I took my own seat, noticing that our good landlady had already set our places with the usual gleaming cutlery atop a spotless white table-cloth, I heard her ascending the stairs. My anticipation of a serving of the roast lamb that I had identified from the aroma emanating from the kitchen was to be temporarily quelled however, for Mrs Hudson entered bearing nothing more than a salver with an envelope upon it.

"How did this come to be here, Mrs Hudson?" Holmes asked as he took the envelope. "Ah, I see that there is no postmark, so I presume it was handed to you upon answering the door."

"Oh no, sir, I found it in the hall. Someone pushed it through the letter-box quietly, or I would have heard."

"Thank you. We will take dinner as soon as it is ready."

As the door closed behind her, he turned the envelope over in his hands, to discover that it was unmarked except for where his name had been scrawled in black ink. After a moment's examination he slit it open with a table knife. A single sheet of paper fell out, and he picked it up by a corner and held it so that we could both read its contents.

Mr Holmes,

You must allow things to take their course. I will let no man prevent it.

The Justice Master.

"So," Holmes smiled thinly, "our mysterious killer is now aware of our pursuit. Whether he is able to curtail its progress remains to be seen."

"Is there anything more to be learned from this?"

He shrugged. "I had identified the sender before I opened the envelope, since the paper is of the same hue and quality as before. He continues to use expensive ink and, judging by the formation of the script and speed with which it appears to have been written, he was in a state of considerable excitement at the time. There is no direct threat here, Watson, but I think we should consider ourselves having been served with a declaration of intent."

"Do you believe we are in danger?"

"I would not ignore the possibility. This man has already demonstrated his willingness to kill anyone who would interfere with his crusade, by his treatment of Mr Croft. Doctor, I recommend that you carry your service weapon at all times, until our investigation is concluded."

"You may depend upon it."

At that point, Mrs Hudson returned with our dinner. I attacked it with relish, as I did the gooseberries and custard that followed, while Holmes displayed his usual scant interest.

Two hours passed, which we spent smoking as we sat in our armchairs. We spoke of what lay ahead of us with some uncertainty, until Holmes rose abruptly and disappeared into his bedroom. He joined me again in a very short time, dressed in the shabby clothes of a workman or dock labourer. On his arm he carried similar apparel.

"Take these to your room and put them on, old fellow, and we will not look out of place."

I complied with this and, hoping that Mrs Hudson would not chance to see us on the stairs, followed my friend into the darkened street. The first hansom that we encountered refused to obey our summons and sped on, out of our sight.

"That, if anything, suggests that our disguises are convincing," Holmes commented.

The next cab halted at our signal, but the driver looked undecided as to whether he should accept our fare.

Holmes was having none of this. He sprang into the hansom and I followed.

"Victoria Dock, cabby," he called, and the horse broke into an immediate trot. We spoke in low voices, Holmes explaining that the Scotland Yard files had contained the whereabouts of the tavern owned by Elizabeth Porter, called 'The Buccaneer'.

Our driver looked surprised when Holmes paid him without either comment or argument. In moments the hansom was lost in the shadows of the poorly-lit street, and we found ourselves quite alone.

"We have already been observed from at least three windows," he murmured. "The slight movement of the curtains is quite sufficient indication."

"I would not care to wander around here for very long, Holmes."

"It is not always such an unfriendly place as it might seem. I have several informants here, who have proven to be useful on numerous occasions."

We reached the end of the street to be faced with the rippling waters of the Thames, illuminated by the light of a full moon. The cobbled street that ran along the quayside was deserted, with upturned small boats here and there and the noise from a variety of drinking establishments loud in our ears as we passed.

Holmes stopped and pointed to a faded sign above us. It was painted with a grotesque image of a scowling pirate with a knife clenched in his teeth and a patch over one eye. In the background I could just make out a galleon with a skull and crossbones flying on its mast.

Without a word, my friend opened the door and we entered. I was immediately taken aback by the thick fog of tobacco and the smell of human sweat. Worse was the noise of many raucous conversations, the crude laughter and the swearing as drunken arguments spent their fury. Somewhere near the end of the room, someone sang hideously.

Every table was occupied, but Holmes' sharp eyes settled on two ruffians near the bar.

"Unless their thirst is not yet quenched, they will be leaving in a moment. Hold yourself ready to claim their seats as they leave them."

Both men rose and shouted something abusive to the man at the bar, who was polishing glasses as he awaited further customers. He smiled faintly and turned away as they staggered past us to the door, laughing like madmen.

"How did you know they would be leaving?" I asked Holmes as we sat down.

"They were drinking from pewter tankards, so I was unable to see the level of beer remaining in them," he replied. "But the angle that they held them as they drank revealed them to be almost empty. So, unless they intended to drink further, they were probably about to leave. I doubt if you are permitted to sit for long, without ordering, in this establishment."

As if to bear him out, I noticed that the barman was staring at us intently. I rose and ordered two pints of his best ale and returned to our table with them. Holmes' eyes were everywhere, as we drank quietly.

"I would think, in a place such as this, that the proprietress, will appear before long. If she is the sort of woman as I suspect, she will wish to observe the evening's merriment personally, to ensure that none of her customers causes any damage and none of the takings find its way into any of her employees' pockets."

"Given the look of them," I said, having already noticed some of the hard-faced men circulating to collect emptied glasses, "I can understand her misgivings."

Before he could reply, a fight erupted at the far end of the room. We watched as drinks, playing cards, and coins were scattered from upturned tables, while two unshaven louts grappled. Their equally roughly turned-out women looked on wondering, it appeared to me, whether to extend the upheaval by attacking each other. This did not occur, as three burly men from the bar, ex-prize fighters I would have said, tore the men apart and conveyed them in an iron grip to the door from where they flung them into the street.

Holmes leaned forward, so that I could hear him above the noise. "Perhaps this occurrence will prove to be to our advantage."

The words were hardly out of his mouth when a door behind the bar was flung open. A tall woman stood there, very still, watching closely as the level of conversation returned to normal and everyone resumed their activities. Clouds of pungent pipe smoke drifted across, fouling the air further.

Her eyes passed over us, and Holmes held up his hand. I saw that he had awaited his opportunity, when the barman and others were occupied elsewhere, to convey to her that we required service. There was an arrogance in her pose, as she strode across to us. She wore a slightly-faded dress of blood-red and as she approached I was able to see that the beautiful face described by Mr Godfrey Carvell was in fact coarsened, that the mouth was a hard line and the eyes glittered without warmth.

"What can I get for you?" Her tone was not welcoming.

"I would like to speak to you for a moment," Holmes said. "Will you not sit with us?"

She remained still. "I have not seen you here before."

"We have not been here before."

She shrugged her shoulders. "What is it that you want?"

I shifted in my chair because her mirthless gaze was causing me some discomfort.

"Nothing more than a little of your time, Mrs Porter."

Her expression hardened. "You are strangers here, yet you know me by name?"

"We are enquiring about an acquaintance of yours," my friend explained.

"And who would that be?"

"Mr Roger Carvell. He was a prisoner when you last saw him, I believe."

Fear crossed her face, before she hissed. "Who are you? If you are from the coppers, I don't know anything. If you have found anything out, I won't pay you to keep quiet." She turned, and gestured, taking in the entire room. "Look around you. If you start trouble, you will find that I am well protected."

"That I do not doubt, neither do I wish to cause you trouble. I would be grateful, however, if you would inform me as to Mr Carvell's whereabouts."

"You talk like a gentleman," she said then. "But I have to tell you, he is dead. He can be of no use to you, now."

"Then perhaps you are acquainted with another, who could suit my purpose just as well."

"And who might I know, like that?"

"Mr Vernon Stark, comes to mind."

She was suddenly very still, and remained silent for several moments. Then she lowered herself into the remaining chair on the opposite side of our table, her eyes never leaving us.

"How do you know that name?"

Holmes regarded her without expression. "It is my business to know such things."

"So you *are* from the coppers?"

"I have not denied that, but it is not so. My name is Sherlock Holmes."

At once her face again took on a fearful look. "I have heard of you, Mr Holmes, and I will tell you only this. If Vernon Stark has upset the law, it is because he has done what he knows to be right. Probably things that they, themselves, should have done. He is not a man to be trifled with, and you would be well advised to leave him alone." She got to her feet. "Finish your drinks and leave, gentlemen. You will find that this is a very rough quarter, if you delay."

She left us then, returning to the bar and speaking to one of the men who was in the act of serving a customer. He nodded and cast a cold look in our direction. I was momentarily distracted by a loud exclamation. Near the middle of the room, a bald and hideously tattooed man had thrown a dice, evidently to his profit. His companions scowled and swore as he claimed his winnings.

"It is time we left this place," I observed. "We can both give good accounts of ourselves, but we would have no chance against so many."

Holmes got to his feet and I followed.

"To remain would be without purpose, in any case. Let us return to Baker Street, taking care that we are not followed, where I will tell you all that I have learned."

Chapter 5 – Loose Ends Are Dangerous

At that hour, in that district, it took Holmes and I some little time to find a hansom. In the end we were fortunate enough to encounter an elderly driver, on his way home after delivering his last fare of the day, who took pity on two workmen who found themselves stranded in the night. My need for sleep was considerable by the time we regained our sitting room, but Holmes seemed as sprightly as ever.

"Before we retire, Watson, I feel that there are a few points we should discuss regarding this evening's little adventure. Allow me to suggest that we do so while enjoying a glass of this excellent port, which I have been intending to sample since its delivery a few days ago."

"I can think of no better way to finish our day."

He poured from the crystal decanter upon the sideboard near the window, and offered a glass to me before seating himself. I tasted the rich, dark liquid and felt calmed by it. We had placed our half-empty glasses on a side-table before, after a moment of silent contemplation, he turned to speak to me.

"It is now obvious, is it not, that Mrs Lilly Porter, nee Bastock is somehow involved in this affair."

"After our conversation with her tonight, I cannot see how it could be otherwise. Her expression on hearing the name 'Vernon Stark' was quite illuminating."

"Indeed. As was her admission that she knew of Roger Carvell's death."

"That was no secret, surely?"

"A secret, no, but his crime, if he did commit one, was old and uninteresting to the public. Lestrade mentioned that the newspapers hardly bothered to report his release, yet Mrs Porter acted as if she was quite familiar with the event. Still, I concede that this is far from conclusive in establishing a connection between her and Stark. Can you recall anything that we could take as more definite?"

In the moment that followed, I searched my memory. The silence from without was disturbed by a carriage driven at speed along Baker Street. Somewhere far-off a dog howled, and then all was quiet.

"She knew enough about Stark to warn us from attempting to interfere with his purpose, but even that does not necessarily mean that she identified him as the Justice Master."

"Excellent, Watson. You seem to have abandoned the bad habit you once had, of reaching conclusions without sufficient evidence. Does anything else of significance strike you?"

"I recall that Mrs Porter appeared to believe us to be blackmailers, before you revealed our identities to her, since she remarked: '*If you have found anything out, I will not pay you to keep quiet*'. That suggests that she is involved in something unlawful, but again it need not be concerned with our investigation."

"My dear fellow," Holmes smiled, "we will make a detective of you yet, for you continue to improve. However, I fear that you have overlooked the most vital point in all this."

"I confess to having observed nothing further."

"Do you recall the experience of Mr Godfrey Carvell, when he actually witnessed the Justice Master, or someone who appeared to be him, at the scene of the murder of Miss Grace LIghtwell?"

I nodded. "I do. He said the murderer threatened him, and had the smile of a madman."

"Which is what we are dealing with here, I have increasingly little doubt. But there was something else that Mr Carvell noticed."

I considered, for an instant, before it came to me. "Of course. A birthmark."

"Precisely. A red birthmark, high on his forehead. Did you not observe that Mrs Porter has a similar mark, in the same place?"

"I did not recognise the blemish as such. I noticed it, yes, but assumed it to be the result of the practice sometimes employed to curl a lady's hair. Hot tongs are used, I believe."

"Yet Mrs Porter's hair was not noticeably curled. Rather, it was straight. This really is too much to be coincidental."

I finished my port and replaced the empty glass. "What then, is your surmise?"

"Is it not obvious? If the man seen by Mr Carvell was our adversary, then Mrs Porter is a blood relative of the Justice Master."

"Then if we were to follow her, might she not eventually lead us to him?"

"That would seem to be an appropriate course of action." Holmes put down his empty glass next to mine. "We will talk more of this tomorrow, Watson, but for now, since I see that sleep is creeping up on you, I will wish you goodnight."

With that he withdrew to his room. I sat for a moment reflecting on our activities of the day and acknowledging that sleep was indeed pressing heavily upon me, before retiring.

I slept fitfully after lying awake listening to Holmes pacing, as he sometimes did while in the midst of a case. As the first rays of the autumn sun lit up the room I arose, to shave with cold water and restore a respectable appearance.

I sat at the table and called for Mrs Hudson, who appeared with a breakfast of bacon and eggs before I had poured my first cup of tea. She cleared away the remains of Holmes' barely-touched food, moments before my friend entered the room with his hat in his hand.

"You have been out already, I see."

He picked up the teapot and filled his cup. "I have laid the bait for our trap. The telegram that I have sent to Mrs Porter will ensure that she departs at once to meet the man who we suspect is behind these killings. We must hurry if we expect to witness this so I beg you, Watson, not to indulge yourself with a second slice of toast. I will procure a hansom while you retrieve your hat and coat."

We arrived at the tavern after Holmes had promised the cabby an extra half-sovereign if he urged his young horse to greater speed. At first I concluded that we were too late for there was some slight commotion outside The Buccaneer, involving four men the worse for drink who had apparently slept on the steps of the establishment. Two of Mrs Porter's staff who we knew from the night before were busily engaged on moving the loafers on, away from where they were obstructing the entry of new customers.

"I fear we may not be in time after all, Holmes," I said as our hansom came to a halt further along the street, "for I feel sure that Mrs Porter would have wished to be present at this incident, trivial as it is. She impressed me as someone who would let nothing happening here pass without her knowledge or participation."

"She does indeed appear to keep a close eye on everything, old fellow, but let us wait and see. Ah, but there she is! She has just emerged wearing a green costume, and must have somehow arranged for the brougham that is approaching to meet her at this time." He rapped on the roof with his stick. "Cabby, we are in pursuit, but be sure to maintain a reasonable distance."

We set off then, the horse being kept at a slow pace with some restraint. From the docks we entered a network of gloomy side-streets of which I knew nothing, although Holmes seemed quite familiar with the district. Here were the streets of the poverty-stricken. Urchins played with makeshift toys while men sat in doorways drinking from bottles of cheap gin, hopelessness clearly written upon their faces. Many of the houses had broken windows, and in all of them brickwork crumbled visibly. A few women in tattered frocks carrying baskets of washing paused to glance at us as we passed, and I realised that this was doubtlessly because carriages were seldom seen here.

Holmes cautioned our driver against drawing too close since, apart from the brougham ahead of us, there was no other traffic in the street. Our quarry turned a corner, losing speed, and my friend immediately called upon our driver to halt. As he did so, we alighted quickly and Holmes paid him with the request that he should not continue in this direction, but should turn his hansom around and return by the same route.

"Why did you ask that of him?" I asked as the hansom passed out of our sight.

"Around that corner ahead of us the way becomes impassable. If the hansom had continued it would have become obvious that we were pursuing the brougham and Mrs Porter would probably take measures to cancel the rendezvous she believes she about to keep. Also, the brougham can go no further, so we are quite near to the meeting place. Come," he gestured to an arched pathway leading to the rear of the row of houses that we faced, "this way!"

He walked briskly beneath the arch and I followed. We found ourselves in a communal wash area, with a small brick structure housing a huge copper bowl at the side of the enclosure. Holmes unhesitatingly approached a wooden gate and wrenched it open. We emerged into a short passage with high walls on either side, and from there into another dilapidated thoroughfare. I marvelled at his knowledge of our city, even of areas such as this where one would surely visit rarely, for his advance was unerring. As we stood in this ruined place, he leaned forward impatiently like a terrier restrained on a leash, looking from side to side and finally settling upon one of the few buildings that appeared to remain standing in a habitable condition.

"There," he pointed. "Keep your service weapon close to hand."

"How can you tell, Holmes? The brougham appears to have already departed."

"It has to be one of the houses in the nearest row, simply because Mrs Porter has had insufficient time to reach the others. You will have noted that the brougham could not have conveyed her further along the street, since the horse would have had difficulty crossing the pit that is probably an unfinished excavation for the repair of a gas main. We are therefore left with the corner dwelling as the only likely structure available to her."

I saw that he was correct, since most of the others were open to the elements. We approached cautiously, to discover that this house too was little more than a façade. Beyond the unlocked front door were the shattered remnants of walls and, further away an unfenced area of what had once been a garden. In the middle of the patchy lawn lay a body, spread out as if crucified.

It was evident that Mrs Porter had died painfully. As we picked our way around the remains of shattered walls and stumbled over fallen beams and ruined furniture, I could see clearly the wire around her neck, the protruding tongue and the horror of her expression.

"See to her, Watson, if there is anything to be done."

Holmes ran on, intending to apprehend the killer or at least to catch sight of him, while I knelt to do what I could for Mrs Porter. It was a futile gesture. I knew before I felt for her pulse that I would find none, the dullness in her eyes made her condition unmistakeable. I shook my head and got to my feet, as Holmes returned.

"This place is like a forest," he said. "There is a large area of ruined properties, beyond these. Our murderer escaped on horseback, too far away for me to see anything other than that he is a man of average height. He must have tethered his mount some distance away, allowing for possible discovery."

"He apparently leaves little to chance." We both glanced at the body. "I fear that there was never any hope for Mrs Porter."

"The wire has cut deeply into her throat, so our murderer is not without strength. As I recall from Lestrade's account, The Justice Master reserves strangulation for his female victims, while using a firearm on all others."

I nodded. "So, he has not deviated from the pattern. It appears that our supposition that Mrs Porter was a relative of his was made in error."

"Not necessarily. Remember, Watson, we are almost certainly dealing with a madman. Is it not so that the reason of such deteriorates gradually?"

"It is believed that this is often so, yes."

Holmes knelt beside the body. "By her expression, she was taken by surprise, which means that she trusted her killer to a degree since he could not have approached by stealth. She does not appear to have scratched him with her rather over-long fingernails, which suggests she was attacked from behind. The ground shows no sign of disturbance, so the altercation was brief, as is indicated by the severity of the wound."

"The jugular vein would have been severed almost immediately," I agreed.

We departed that place soon after, Holmes resolving to send a telegram to Lestrade on our way back to Baker Street. In fact, we walked at least a mile before we were able to engage a passing hansom to return us to our lodgings, and on arrival discovered that the morning held one more surprise for us.

The letter, which Mrs Hudson had placed on a side-table in the hall to await our return, read:

Mr Holmes,

You go too far. Nothing will deter me. You have now seen that I am prepared to pursue to the end the task which is my destiny. Turn aside, while you still can. I will be watching.

"There is no signature," Holmes observed. "Apparently the Justice Master no longer considers it necessary to identify himself to us."

"Also, from the words, 'you have seen that I am prepared to pursue....', it would seem that he is confirming that the killing of someone related to him matters little, if it furthers his purpose."

"That is speculation, Watson, but not unlikely. The implication of the last two sentences, however, is unmistakeable."

"It appears that he regards our investigation as something of a challenge."

"Or as the beginning of a duel. Presumably, he murdered Mrs Porter to prevent her from disclosing information regarding him to us or to the official force. Possibly he had developed a mistrust of her, and was either watching the tavern or present within it, last night."

"If he was there, she gave no indication of it."

"None, it is true, but then she would be unlikely to, on learning of the reason for our presence."

"Once again, it becomes difficult to proceed."

To my surprise, my friend smiled. "Indeed, but perhaps that situation may be temporary. I suggest, old fellow, that after consuming a sufficient portion of Mrs Hudson's lamb stew, we discuss the matter while enjoying a leisurely smoke."

Our luncheon over, we settled ourselves into our armchairs and Holmes produced a box of South American cigars. We each made our selection and lit them from a vesta, drawing on the fragrant smoke deeply. It was then that he leaned back in his chair, thoughtfully blowing rings into the air above.

"I wonder how Lestrade is faring, with his investigation," I said after a while, to break the silence.

"It is unlikely, I think, that he has achieved much progress. Had he done so, he would have been unable to resist sharing it with us, as much out of pride as to further our enquiries."

"And Mr Grantly-Knight?"

"He cannot continually observe us closely, but he is able to do so quite easily where the official force is concerned. I do not doubt that he has been something of a nuisance to our good inspector, constantly seeking to learn not only of his advancement towards the solving of this case, but also to glean anything that might have been learned from ourselves. I have said that I will keep him informed, but only when I have a great deal more to report than at present."

He lapsed into silence again, quietly pondering as we finished our cigars. As I extinguished the remnants of mine in an ash-tray he turned to me, his expression sombre.

"I have considered the question of our progress at length, Watson, and have arrived at a solution. It will, I fear, impose heavily upon certain resources that I have built over the years, but no matter. It appears that the Justice Master now kills, if not at random then when anyone poses the slightest threat to his purpose, and is on the brink of losing control of his obsession. Make no mistake, this man has a lust for killing. His supposed reason, that the law has dealt too leniently with his victims, is merely an excuse to himself to justify his actions. We therefore cannot allow this rampage of murder to continue on the streets of the capital. I have formulated a strategy which is likely to ensnare him, but the co-operation of the official force is essential. Our killer doubtlessly desires a further victim at the earliest opportunity. Very well, we will see if we can supply him with one."

Chapter 6 – A Trap is Set

Our second visit to Scotland Yard had a more fortunate result. On this occasion we encountered Inspector Lestrade as we entered the building, and soon found ourselves seated before his overcrowded desk.

"I am sorry to confess, gentlemen, that we have made little progress in this case," he said dejectedly. "The body of Mrs Porter has been taken to the mortuary for examination, but there is little mystery as to the cause of her death."

"But too much as to the identity of her murderer," Holmes observed. "It would appear that he now kills for reasons other than, as he sees it, the failure of the law to punish adequately certain ones who have fallen foul of it."

"I have arranged for more constables to patrol our streets at night. Every beat is set so that it crosses over at least one other, every fifteen minutes. Apart from intensifying our investigation, I cannot see what else can be done."

Holmes nodded. "Excellent precautions, Lestrade, but I have devised something more. If you will assist me, I believe I can provide us with an opportunity to apprehend the Justice Master within a day or two."

"If you have a suggestion, I will be pleased to hear it."

"Tell me first, who is the next prisoner to be released, having avoided execution? I recall that you mentioned previously, that something of the sort is to occur in the new year."

The little detective consulted some papers which he took from a drawer. "Yes, I have it here. Miss Miriam Hedgely is likely to regain her freedom in January. She was found guilty of the murder of her uncle and was due to hang, but a neighbour confessed on his death-bed recently."

"Yet she remains a prisoner?" I queried.

"Pending a new investigation to verify the confession, yes. You see, doctor, it would not be the first time that such an admission was made when a dying man sought to falsely exonerate a condemned man or woman for various reasons. However, I am told that both the investigation and the formalities are expected to be completed by January."

"Doubtlessly the newspapers have already revealed this to the public." Holmes said with certainty.

Lestrade scowled. "They have, although there was no official release of the information. It is suspected that someone within the prison was paid to disclose it."

"That may have occurred to our advantage. This is what I propose. Imagine for a moment that Miss Hedgely was released immediately, and the dailies announced not only this but where she is to live. Is it not likely that the Justice Master, with his obsession for destroying those who have cheated the hangman, will seek to claim her as his next victim?"

"It would be indeed, Mr Holmes, if it were possible to bring about such a situation." The incredulity in the inspector's voice was poorly concealed. "But consider, if you will, the difficulties. To begin, authority would have to be obtained for an early release. Then Miss Hedgely would have to agree to expose herself to certain danger." He smiled faintly. "After serving a term of imprisonment, apparently unjustly, she is unlikely to be keen to offer us her help."

He looked faintly pleased at having raised objections so easily to Holmes' plan. A moment of silence descended upon us before I heard running footsteps in the corridor, presumably in response to a violent commotion at the front of the building. The inspector glanced towards the door, but made no move to investigate.

"I have not yet made myself clear, Lestrade," Holmes said quietly. "Pray allow me to do so."

"Of course, but I cannot see how…."

"It is not such a difficult problem as it first appears. Firstly, the matter of securing authority. This is where I require your assistance, but only to enable Watson, myself and one other to enter the prison yard at Holloway. Further, the participation of Miss Miriam Hedgely is not required."

The official detective's eyes narrowed. "Your intentions elude me, Mr Holmes, but you have produced good results before now. How, then, do you intend to proceed?"

"As I have mentioned before, on occasion, I have a considerable number of acquaintances within the capital. I once gave some trifling aid to the manager of a theatrical troupe, whose only child was kidnapped, and his gratitude was without limit. I intend to confront him with the likeness of Miss Hedgerly, if you would be good enough to supply a photograph from your files, and request that he introduce me to someone who not only resembles her, but is willing to undertake some risk."

"I have no doubt that this could turn out successfully," Lestrade said after a moment's silence, "but Scotland Yard cannot be seen to endanger the life of a member of the public. No, I fear I must decline your most interesting suggestion, Mr Holmes."

"The lady in question would enter into the arrangement voluntarily, naturally. I will of course attend to any payments or further arrangements."

Lestrade stared at us without expression but I could see that he was thinking furiously.

"Very well," he said at length. "The Yard has, after all, no power to govern the actions of anyone save those breaking the law. If I can obtain such permission, I take it that it is so that the imposter can be seen leaving the prison, to add to the deception?"

"Precisely. Also, the newspapers must be notified with discretion. The 'release' will quickly become common knowledge, and the Justice Master will act."

"Where do you intend that she should stay, while awaiting his attempt?"

"I have in mind rooms in Brick Lane, Whitechapel. Their position is such that they can be guarded from several directions simultaneously. Watson and myself will be close by, but it may be as well to have others watching from a short distance."

The detective's bulldog-like face clouded as he considered, then he came to a decision.

"I will do what I can to reserve several constables for concealment within the area, Mr Holmes. They could perhaps use nearby public houses from which to watch the place. If my memory serves me aright, The Frying Pan is closest."

"Capital, Lestrade!" Holmes cried approvingly. "In addition, there may be other rooms close by that can be rented temporarily for our purpose. Watson and I will return to Baker Street now, to begin our own arrangements. I will keep you informed, and would be grateful if you would send notification when you have consulted the prison authorities."

We left the inspector then, to return to our lodgings. Holmes requested our cabby to stop once, in order to send a telegram to someone whose name I did not recognise.

I contained my curiosity until we were seated at our table, awaiting dinner.

"Who is Mr Edward Pillinger, Holmes?" I asked. "I cannot recall your previous mention of him."

My friend inclined his head, listening as Mrs Hudson ascended the stairs. "He is the owner of the theatrical troupe that I spoke of while we were with Lestrade. Our hopes of apprehending the Justice Master may depend upon his reply."

I had no chance to ask more before Mrs Hudson entered, carrying steaming plates of curried pork. Unusually, Holmes cleared his plate before I did justice to my ample portion, but he refused the steamed pudding which followed. It was as we were finishing our coffee, that the door-bell rang to announce that the answer to his telegram had arrived. Our good landlady brought it to him and cleared away the dinner things, as we retired to our armchairs. He placed the unopened envelope on a side-table, as he filled his clay pipe with coarse shag from the Persian slipper which he kept near the fire-place.

"Now, Watson," he said as he blew out a cloud of smoke and slit open the envelope with a thumb-nail. "we shall see in which direction our little snare is to be set."

I put a light to my own pipe, watching his face as his eyes swept over the contents of the message. By the lightening of his expression, I knew at once that the news was good.

"Excellent!" he exclaimed, flinging the telegram to the floor. "Mr Pillinger will be pleased to see us at ten o'clock tomorrow morning. He indicates that he understands my request and will have on hand several young women who may be suitable. Watson, the game is indeed afoot."

After that we spent a few hours in pleasant conversation and recollection, and retired early.

When I sat down to breakfast the following morning, Holmes was holding a photograph which he handed to me at once.

"Lestrade was as good as his word. This was delivered by hand."

I took the picture from him. A dark-haired young woman with a strong and not unattractive face looked back at me. Her eyes and expression were full of determination and, I thought, outrage. If this poor girl had, as Lestrade indicated, been imprisoned unjustly, then little else could be expected.

"She does not look to me like a murderess, Holmes."

"But how *would* such a woman look?" He queried with a smile. "As always, Watson, you allow yourself to be deceived by the outward appearance. One day I will tell you of Priscilla Ghent, an American visitor to our shores with a face that would have rivalled that of Venus. I was able to discover that she was fleeing her own country to escape punishment for the killing of five men, in order to inherit their assets. She was eventually returned there but the point is, as I have said before, that the female sex cannot be trusted. Even the best of them are deceptive by nature."

I have never agreed with Holmes on this, so I did not pursue his assertion. Instead, I reminded him:

"In the case of Miss Hedgerly, her guilt has already been disproven."

"That may be the case, but the official investigation has yet to be concluded. However, I see that the time by which we must leave is approaching, and therefore I will not delay you in finishing your eggs. As for me, a cup of strong coffee will suffice."

Shortly after, we hurriedly put on our hats and coats. As we boarded a passing hansom, I heard my friend instruct the driver: "Wych Street, near The Strand. The Olympic theatre."

We made good progress, until we reached The Strand. Holmes shifted impatiently in his seat as we were forced to lose speed by an extraordinary number of hansoms and four-wheelers queueing ahead. After a moment he opened the door and stepped down, onto the road.

"Come, Watson. I have no wish to be late."

"But we are not in sight of the Olympic, as yet."

Nevertheless, I followed his lead and left the cab. He handed up some coins to the cabby and proceeded to lead me through one of the vilest alleys imaginable, its air thick with the stench of decay, until we emerged into Wych Street to be confronted by our destination.

We strode between the narrow pillars into the foyer, where a handsome, middle-aged woman waited, evidently expecting us. After greetings had been exchanged, she guided us down a short corridor before knocking upon a plain door of dark wood. A voice from within bade us enter, and she announced us before withdrawing discreetly. At the far end of the large room was a stage, and I realised that this was where rehearsals were held, and possibly selections, while the remaining space was taken up by enough chairs to contain an audience of twenty or thirty. Sitting about ten yards away was a man of bulky physique with a magnificent handlebar moustache. He quickly got to his feet and approached us.

"Mr Holmes, how good it is to see you again." They shook hands before he turned to me. "And you, sir, must be Doctor Watson, who turns Mr Holmes' exploits into such thrilling tales."

I affirmed my identity, and we also shook hands. Holmes appeared slightly embarrassed (or I may have imagined it) by this reference to his past activities, but this quickly faded as we took our seats.

"I am indebted to you for accommodating me, Mr Pillinger," Holmes said.

"Not at all," came the jovial reply, "for it is I who will always be indebted to you for the safe return of my little Ellie, who is not so little anymore. I gave some thought to the contents of your message, and I have selected six girls of spirit who, after my guarded explanation, are prepared to participate even to the risk of their lives." He paused, fingering his moustache. "I should mention that they require substantially more than their usual wage for this service, and that I will bear all costs. No, Mr Holmes, do not object, for I will have none of it."

"Very well," my friend replied. "You have my heartfelt thanks."

Mr Pillinger nodded. "I have chosen these as the most likely to agree to the conditions, but of course I have no way of selecting according to appearance. If you can now provide a likeness of the lady you wish to substitute, we can proceed with our final choice."

Holmes produced the photograph that he had shown to me earlier, and Mr Pillinger studied it closely.

"Very well," he said at length. "Let us see."

He clapped his hands, and at once six young women appeared and paraded across the stage before us. They positioned themselves a few feet apart and some of them smiled faintly. Each was dressed in a respectable fashion and had her own features of attraction but, alas, none of them resembled Miriam Hedgerly. I glanced at Holmes, and saw that his disappointment was evident.

"Do you perhaps have others to choose from?" he asked.

Mr Pillinger appeared astounded. "Why should that be necessary, sir? I confess that my selection was, for the most part, a guess as far as appearance is concerned, but this little picture tells me at once that I have made no error." He hesitated. "Ah, I see, of course. You gentlemen are viewing the problem as you see it, which is to be expected. To me it is different. I am thinking as I would if I were preparing one of these ladies for a show, for a performance as a preconceived character. What do you think of the girl standing third from the right? I believe that she was made for this role."

I peered through the half-light, at the illuminated figures standing patiently on the stage. "I regret, I cannot see a resemblance."

Holmes shook his head. "I must concur."

"Yet I tell you, she is the one to do this." Mr Pillinger laughed. "It must seem unlikely to you, being not of the profession, but I will demonstrate. Down the road from here, in Newcastle Street, is a tavern, The Flying Horse. I suggest that you gentlemen spend a pleasant hour there, perhaps enjoying a pint of strong ale, before returning here. Then you will see the result of the attentions of a skilled make-up artist. Do you agree?"

Holmes and I did so, in unison.

"You can all leave, with my thanks, save Jenny," he shouted then. At Mr Pillinger's instruction, the ladies turned and marched off-stage with almost military precision. The remaining girl stood waiting, as we left.

The prospect of an early luncheon appealed to us, so it was with cheese and pickles to accompany our ale that we sat in the Flying Horse shortly afterwards.

I looked slowly around the bar-room, through the smoke. "This place seems to have a strange clientele, Holmes," I observed.

He smiled. "Theatrical people are often unconventional. You may recall that I had experience of them, some years ago."

"Indeed. Why then, did you not agree with Mr Pillinger's assessment?"

"As you know there have been many occasions when I have been obliged to adopt a disguise. However, I have never been confronted with the task of altering the appearance of a woman. It seems to me to be quite different to that of working upon oneself, or upon another man, but we will soon see, for my pocket-watch tells me that we can return now."

Ten minutes later we found ourselves in the theatre once more, this time in the cramped office of Mr Pillinger. We entered to find him at his desk, one of the three chairs before it being occupied by a woman. She sat with her back to us and did not turn around until we had closed the door, when he gave a signal with a movement of his hand.

I recall clearly his expression of satisfaction as she stood and faced us, as well as my own amazement. Holmes appeared to be as astounded as I have rarely seen him.

"Good day, gentlemen," Miss Miriam Hedgerly said.

Chapter 7 - A Narrow Escape

I stared at her, completely at a loss for words.

"Clearly, your make-up artist and yourselves are masters of your profession," Holmes said quietly.

Mr Pillinger gave a little bow, and the girl smiled at our surprise.

"Holmes, this is fantastic," I said as I regained my speech. "I have seldom seen such a transformation."

"I trust that you are aware," Holmes said to the girl, "of the dangers involved here. Pray think carefully, even now, before you begin to participate."

She looked back at us with earnest eyes. "Mr Pillinger has shared with me such information as he has been given. It took but little thought, considering your profession, Mr Holmes, to arrive at the conclusion that I am to be used to assist in the capture of some notorious criminal. I have read of several murders in London, lately."

"You are indeed an exceptional girl," my friend observed. "Be assured that Doctor Watson and myself, as well as the official force, will never be far away from you. Allow me to enlighten you as to some details...."

He went on to describe the rudiments of our intended course of action. When he had finished the girl's expression was unchanged. She showed no sign of doubt or fear.

"Gentlemen," she said when all had been told to her, "I fully understand. For now I will continue my profession under the guidance of Mr Pillinger, but will hold myself ready to assist you whenever you may call."

"Our grateful thanks to you," Holmes responded. "When I have heard from Scotland Yard that we are clear to begin I will communicate with Mr Pillinger by telegraph, and he will doubtlessly inform you immediately."

"Then I will await your summons."

We took our leave shortly after, and were fortunate enough to encounter a hansom that had delivered its fare on the corner of Drury Lane. Holmes sat in deep thought with his head upon his chest during the journey back to Baker Street, and to the best of my recollection spoke only once.

"That is a very brave young lady, Watson. We must exercise great caution during this escapade of ours, so as not to fail her. I have little doubt that the Justice Master will strike swiftly, once he reads that 'Miriam Hedgerly' is at liberty."

"Mr Pillinger too, has aided us greatly in this."

He nodded thoughtfully. "Indeed."

Two days passed, during which Holmes despatched two telegrams in answer to the contents of his morning post, and conducted several chemical experiments with results that seemed to please him. As for me, I visited my practice briefly, to ensure that the inexperienced young locum was in no difficulty, took solitary walks and caught up with the growing pile of medical journals that again awaited my attention.

It was as the light faded on the second evening that, returning from walking among a carpet of golden leaves in Hyde Park and anticipating a glass of port with Holmes before

Mrs Hudson's steak and kidney pudding, that I realised at once that something had occurred to advance our investigation.

Holmes wore a grim smile and exhibited the nervous demeanour that I knew of old. It meant that something had excited him. His eyes glittered, and his jaw was set.

"Lestrade has been here, Watson. The governor of Holloway has given his permission, but only if we are accompanied by a member of the official force. Come, old fellow, we will walk to the Post Office together, and I will give you the details on the way. I will send word to Mr Pillinger, and request that Jenny Farrel is despatched by the early train. She should arrive well before luncheon tomorrow."

As I walked with him I fancied that I could feel the repressed energy that I saw in his movements. I learned little more, only that it was to be Lestrade who accompanied us to Holloway, which was to be expected. The telegram despatched, we returned to Baker street at a leisurely pace, I anxious to quell the pangs of hunger and Holmes apparently indifferent to them.

"After we have eaten I will be going out," he told me then. "No, Watson, you need not accompany me. I am going to number 3, Brick Lane, to ensure that everything is prepared for the installation of Miss Farrel, and to examine the immediate area. I am determined to leave little to chance."

Accordingly, he left our lodgings with his meal half-finished and before Mrs Hudson had yet to clear away its remains. When I had eaten my fill I took to my usual armchair after requesting her to light the fire, as an autumn coolness had replaced the warmth of the day. After a cigar and the glass of port that I had promised myself earlier, I lowered my newspaper and began to dwell upon our situation.

It did not seem to me that our plan could misfire. Holmes and I would be armed and waiting for the Justice Master to put in an appearance at the rooms in Brick Lane. Any caller would immediately become the focus of our attention and suspicion, and Miss Farrel would be well guarded at all times. Holmes and I would take turns in keeping watch, and Lestrade's constables would be on hand to observe anyone approaching from any direction. I was concerned only about the length of this vigil, for our adversary might reason that his task would be easier when some days had passed – he might consider it likely that our guard would then be lowered. Not that I would expect that of Holmes, who I had known to deprive himself of sleep for days on occasion, but I had less confidence in my own powers. Finally, I resolved to steel myself to give of my best, and then I must have fallen asleep because I became aware of my friend taking the half-empty glass from my limp hand as the chimes of a distant church clock reached me faintly.

"It would be better, Watson, if you refrained from staining Mrs Hudson's carpet with wine." As I shook myself awake he took off his hat and coat and assured me: "All is now prepared. I suggest we retire without delay, since the early train arrives at Paddington at nine o'clock. Miss Farrel will be already in the guise of Miss Miriam Hedgerly, so we must be on our guard from the moment we meet her. From the station, we will go directly to Holloway."

I had barely acknowledged this, before he wished me a brisk goodnight and disappeared into his room. In my own bed, I lay awaiting sleep for some time. Holmes, I thought, must have arranged things to his satisfaction, since I could hear no sounds of him pacing his room. I began once again to review our intentions, seeking to be absolutely certain that they had no flaw, but then weariness again overwhelmed me and I slept soundly until I awoke to a dull and dismal day.

Breakfast was over quickly. Holmes had seized his coat and handed me mine before I had finished my last slice of toast. We crossed Baker Street to engage a hansom that stood awaiting a fare, and were on our way to Paddington in moments.

We awaited the train with a small crowd surrounding us. Holmes' eyes were everywhere. From the moment we left the hansom his wariness had been evident to me, but only because I knew his ways. I could see no one who appeared suspicious, but several times I sensed a tenseness in his posture which quickly vanished as he decided that the subject of his scrutiny was not, after all, a threat.

A loud voice, the station-master or a guard, announced that the train's arrival was imminent, and already I could hear the distant whistle and sense the vibrations from the track.

"Any moment now, Watson," Holmes murmured as, an instant later, the engine hurtled into sight amid a cloud of smoke and with its brakes screaming.

We stepped back, in order to take in as many coaches as we could as the doors were swung open. Twice I found myself on the point of approaching alighting young women, but he placed a hand on my shoulder and shook his head. Then a girl in a dark blue costume appeared, wearing a wide-brimmed hat and a veil, and Holmes helped her onto the platform while I took her single small trunk.

"Good morning, gentlemen," she said before either of us could say a word. "I have answered your summons, as promised."

Holmes smiled. "Our thanks to you again, Miss Farrel. May I suggest that you retain your veil until we leave

Holloway. Your exposure will last but a short time, and then you can resume your normal self."

With that we made our way from the platform, leaving the station to find Inspector Lestrade awaiting us in a four-wheeler.

After we had introduced Miss Farrel, we began to discuss the task that lay ahead of us. Lestrade listened patiently to Holmes' observations and instructions, as did she. We immersed ourselves in the refining of our intended actions, vaguely aware of our passage through backstreets and main thoroughfares, until the horse was reined in and the prison gates confronted us.

Two uniformed guards stared at us suspiciously, the elder man approaching and asking our business there. On Lestrade's reply a signal was given to the remaining guard, who rapped upon the gates with his truncheon. A moment later, we entered the grim enclosure and the gates closed behind us.

"You understand, gentlemen, that you must depart within half an hour," the elder guard, having followed our carriage in, reminded us.

Lestrade looked questioningly at Holmes, who explained. "That should be sufficient. I have arranged that the representatives of the press will arrive in about ten minutes, if they are prompt. Pray alert us then."

"Very well, sir." The guard returned to his post outside.

"You have timed this with little to spare, Holmes," I observed.

"That was essential, since Miss Farrel's exposure as Miss Hedgerly must be kept to a minimum. All that is required is that the reporters are allowed a fleeting glance, enough to convince them that the prisoner is now at liberty, so that the evening editions will feature it prominently." He paused as the sounds of arriving carriages reached us from beyond the gates, and one of the guards again rapped out a signal. "They are a little early. I would be obliged if you will lift your veil now, Miss Farrel."

She did so and the striking resemblance to the absent Miss Hedgerly again astonished me. Lestrade also appeared astounded, but made no comment. Holmes looked out with a wary expression as the gates opened again and we moved slowly into the street. The group stared at us intently as they scribbled in their notebooks. Miss Farrel leaned forward in her seat, so that they could not fail to observe her features clearly. When we had passed by, and left behind also the waiting hansoms, she resumed her former position and looked at Holmes and Lestrade with an amused smile.

"Well, did I perform well, gentlemen?"

"You did so most adequately," Holmes confirmed.

"I am sure that you did, Miss," the inspector agreed. "I hope our murderer reads the newspapers."

During the journey I noticed that my friend was again watchful for any hansom or carriage following. After a while, apparently satisfied, he looked out at our changing surroundings less often. A short while before we arrived at Whitechapel High Street, Lestrade requested that the driver rein in the horse for him to alight, assuring us as he did so that the promised constables would shortly be at their posts not far from us. We watched him disappear into the dull labyrinth shortly before we found ourselves in Osborn Street, and thence to its continuation, Brick Lane.

I could tell from the cabby's demeanour that he was uncomfortable, and I could sympathise – this was not a district one would frequent by choice. Holmes paid him generously and, after we had watched the carriage depart, he produced a key and opened the unpainted door for us to enter.

I saw at once that he had gone to considerable lengths to ensure our comfort. The place was clean, certainly, and the furniture appeared new. I noticed a shelf of books and a carafe of wine. A bottle of fine cognac stood near two large hampers of cold food. It seemed to me that, as long as we remained watchful, our stay here would prove to be less of an endurance than I had imagined.

Holmes placed his hand on my arm. "Kindly remain here with Miss Farrel, Watson, with your hand on your revolver."

I complied, and we watched as he inspected every corner of the room and the small kitchen beyond, before cautiously ascending the stairs to the rooms above. Clearly, my friend did not take the threat of the Justice Master lightly, and intended that all risks to our persons should be kept to a minimum.

"All is as it should be," he announced on his return. "Miss Farrel, if you wish you may now remove your disguise. Were it not for the possibility that you could be observed leaving the premises, I would recommend that you return to Mr Pillinger. I regret that you are exposed to further danger."

She turned to him with a defiant light in her eyes. "This man is a threat to the people of our city, Mr Holmes, not least to some who have paid for their crimes. I am neither afraid nor unwilling to assist in his capture."

With that she took to the stairs, and I carried her trunk after her. When she was installed in one of the rooms I returned to Holmes, who was peering out of the wide window into the street at a carefully-selected angle.

"That is a brave girl," I remarked.

"A woman of spirit," he agreed.

She reappeared after a short while, having freed herself of all traces of Miss Miriam Hedgerly. I confess to have been again startled by the transformation and, as well as marvelling at the skill of Mr Pillinger's make-up artist, I found myself glad to reaffirm that the true appearance of Miss Farrel was considerably more attractive.

The hour for luncheon was upon us, and we dined upon newly-baked bread and cold ham. I made a note to enquire of Holmes later how he had arranged for our food and the obvious extensive cleaning and furnishing of our temporary residence, but I knew from past experience that he would answer with vague references to his varied contacts throughout the capital.

We spent the afternoon in conversation. As we grew accustomed to Miss Farrel's presence, the talk flowed more freely. Holmes, in fact, delighted her by recounting veiled versions of several of our past adventures, and one instance when he had solved a complicated affair while living in Montague Street. During this time it did not escape my notice that his eyes strayed often to the window, and that he regularly inclined his head in a listening manner.

As the light began to fade I rose to draw the heavy curtains as he lit the lamps. Outside was a dull, deserted street and I observed that Lestrade's constables, if they waited nearby, had concealed themselves well. Something then arrested my attention, and I realised that there had been a change out there. I peered again, into the rapidly disappearing scene.

"Holmes, it looks as if a thick fog is descending."

He joined me at the window. "So it would appear. If the Justice Master chooses tonight to pay us a visit, it will be to his advantage."

"It will certainly conceal him well," Miss Farrel observed.

"You must try not to be anxious," I advised her. "We are here to protect you."

She smiled. "Gentlemen, there is perhaps something that I should have told you."

Holmes and I watched as she took a small pearl-handled pistol from her purse.

"Do not be alarmed," she said. "My father, an army officer, taught me to shoot during my childhood. Where we lived then, in India, it was a wise precaution. You see, you must not imagine that I am helpless."

Holmes and I looked at each other in surprise.

"Pray do not produce that weapon unless your life is threatened," he advised grimly. "To handle firearms excessively is exceedingly dangerous."

She nodded and replaced it in her purse.

Shortly afterwards we dined, this time on cold roast beef.

"A poor substitute for a hot meal," Holmes remarked to Miss Farrel, "but it will suffice for now."

She shook her head. "Not so, sir. I have gone to my bed on many a night with lesser food in my stomach, sometimes with none at all. I doubt if there is anyone in all London, who has chosen the acting profession and fared better at the beginning."

Holmes made no reply, but returned to the window and again peered out. From where I sat I could see that the fog had already obscured our view of the opposite side of the street. It swirled and thickened as we watched, and a feeling of grim foreboding all but overcame me.

"Do not despair, Watson," he said as if he had read my mind. "Now that we have eaten we can continue our reminiscences for the amusement of Miss Farrel, perhaps with an accompanying glass of brandy."

Thus we passed the evening. No sound reached us from outside, partially because of the deadening effects of the choking brown mass that now hung everywhere. By the time ten o'clock approached, both she and I had grown weary and would soon have retired, but Holmes suddenly stiffened in his chair in the manner of an animal that has become aware of imminent danger.

"Did you hear something, Holmes?" I enquired.

He was silent for a moment, listening further before answering. "There were running footsteps outside, a few seconds ago. Two people, I think."

We crowded around the window as he lifted the edge of the curtain. The fog was an impenetrable barrier. We could see nothing beyond it. Holmes inclined his head, his sharp ears straining, before the dull report of a gunshot reached us, and then another.

My friend drew his revolver, as we heard an agonised cry. "I am going out there, Watson. Look after Miss Farrel."

Immediately she began to protest that this was unnecessary, and I attempted to dissuade him.

"Holmes, I beg you not to do this. We are safe here, it is easier to defend this house than to risk being attacked or shot in this fog."

But he had gone before I finished my entreaty. After making certain that the door was securely closed I looked out again, but there was nothing to be seen but the featureless cloud that surrounded us.

Miss Farrel, I think, was about to speak when a terrible crash from the direction of the kitchen arrested our attention. I drew my service weapon and instructed her to remain, before cautiously advancing towards the rear of the house. I entered the kitchen to see at once that the outer door had been caved in. A heavy iron bar lay on the threshold, at the feet of a masked figure with a garrotte wound around his hands. At the sight of me he immediately attempted to disentangle himself and quickly succeeded in doing so, producing a pistol with lightning speed. I began to shout a warning, but he levelled his weapon so that I had little choice but to fire. His pistol fell to the floor and he cried out in pain before, seeing that I had now lowered my own firearm, disappearing into the fog leaving the foulest of oaths hanging in the air.

I peered out into the murk, but pursuit was hopeless. Holmes had charged me with Miss Farrel's protection, and I knew that he would be greatly displeased if I ventured out. I returned to the living-room, where she awaited me anxiously.

"Doctor Watson, are you hurt?"

"No," I reassured her, "but I suggest you retrieve your pistol and keep it by you while I see what has become of Holmes. The kitchen door has been smashed in, but I think our adversary has fled. For safety's sake, remain alert."

After ensuring that Miss Farrel stood away from the kitchen, I opened the front door and stepped out, peering into the fog.

"Holmes! Are you there? Holmes!"

My cries were lost in the fog, dull sounds as if I had shouted into a closed room, and were met with silence. Moments later, two vague figures gradually took shape before me, and my friend's voice answered.

"You need not concern yourself, Watson. We are safe."

Holmes and Lestrade emerged to stand next to me, as a police whistle shrilled a short distance away.

"Constable Short will soon summon help, Mr Holmes. We can safely repair to the house," the inspector said before they entered.

"What happened out there?" I enquired urgently.

"Constable Greening and I saw a figure approaching the house," Lestrade answered. "He seems to have sensed our approach, for he turned and fired. The constable went down, but I was able to return fire. I believe that I hit the intruder, but in this fog I could not tell."

"I must see to the constable at once!" I exclaimed. I quickly retraced my steps and retrieved my medical bag from the corner where I had left it close at hand, before presenting myself.

"It was to our right where I met Lestrade," Holmes explained, "so if we move to our left we have the best chance of coming upon the constable, and possibly his assailant."

I ensured that Miss Farrel had her pistol to hand before we set out into the fog, keeping close to each other. For some minutes we wandered without any break in the surrounding mass, before Holmes suddenly gripped my arm.

"There! This way, Watson."

With Lestrade close behind us, we advanced on the stricken body of the constable.

We drew nearer, until we were able to see him more clearly.

"He's alive!" cried Lestrade. "I saw him move."

We reached the officer, and I conducted a quick examination. He gripped his stomach and groaned loudly, but there was no blood.

Lestrade leaned over for a closer look. "Where is he injured, doctor? He appears in great pain, but he is not bleeding."

"Look at his metal belt buckle," Holmes directed. "It is grossly misshapen. By an extraordinary chance the bullet struck it and ricocheted, but did not enter the constable's body. Nevertheless, the force must have knocked him off his feet, and possibly there are internal injuries. Do you agree, Watson?"

"Absolutely. It will be some time before help arrives, especially in this fog. A dose of laudanum will help to kill the pain until then."

I administered this immediately, then Holmes and Lestrade carried Constable Greening into the house where Miss Farrel, having laid down her weapon, insisted on taking charge.

"We must go out again," Holmes said to Lestrade and myself. "I saw blood on the pavement, a short distance from where the constable lay. It cannot be his, so it is likely that his assailant either lies wounded or has left a trail for us to follow."

Closing the door firmly we set off in the same direction, Holmes studying the ground as best he could with limited visibility. Moments after we came upon the place where Constable Greening had fallen, we were able to dimly discern another body lying prone and covered with blood.

We approached cautiously, but the precaution was needless. The man was quite dead and his pistol lay several feet away. I saw that he was hideously tattooed, with a dragon depicted on either side of his face and a snake across his bald head.

"Your aim was good, Lestrade," Holmes remarked.

"We will hear no more from the Justice Master, I think."

"Holmes!" I exclaimed as the memory came back to me. "This is not the Justice Master. I remember this man in the tavern, The Buccaneer."

He nodded. "At the dice table."

"That does not exclude him, surely?" Lestrade protested.

I shook my head. "I have not yet had the opportunity to tell you what transpired in the house, at the same time as this man appeared."

"I recall hearing another gunshot," the inspector said. "At the time, I dismissed it as an echo."

"It would be best, I think, to return to the house," Holmes suggested. "There we can discuss this as we enjoy the restorative effects of a glass of brandy. No one will see this man's body in this fog, and we can inform the official force when reinforcements arrive. I take it that no one was injured during the exchange that you witnessed, Watson?"

"No one except the Justice Master himself," I agreed as we retraced our steps. "I believe that I wounded him, but not fatally."

When we were settled I recounted the occurrence, showing Holmes and Lestrade the ruined door after ensuring that Constable Greening now slept deeply. Miss Farrel's manner was now considerably quieter. Possibly, I surmised, because of the alarming events she had witnessed.

"I must say, Watson," Holmes commented, "that you acted with extraordinary presence of mind. It is unfortunate though, that the Justice Master's wound failed to prevent his escape."

"The fog served him well," I recalled. "It hid him from my sight before I could fire again."

"Did you see his face?" Lestrade asked.

I shook my head. "He wore a mask, and a wide-brimmed hat was pulled down over his brow."

"Unfortunate," Holmes said again as he put down his empty glass, "but it will do harm, I think, if I examine the area to see whether any trace of him remains."

In the kitchen he discovered a lantern which he lit and carried before him through the ruined kitchen door. The swirling fog engulfed him instantly, and the glow from the lantern quickly faded. Twice I called out to him, into the dark silence, but my cries went unanswered. After almost twenty minutes his tall form emerged, reappearing suddenly in a ghost-like manner.

"Did you discover anything?" I enquired.

"Disappointingly little." He doused the lantern and placed it upon the kitchen table. "All I could deduce is that our adversary is a man of average height and normal build. These things were easily discernible from the footprints in the soft soil. That he is of no great height is suggested also by the fact that the low wooden strut above the gate to the rear of the garden shows no sign of blood from a collision. Otherwise this would almost certainly have occurred as a fleeing man hurried through, unable to avoid it because of the fog."

"It seems then," Lestrade said, "that the intention was for the tattooed man to distract the intention of the occupants while the Justice Master entered the house from the rear. We cannot be sure if they believed Miss Farrel to be alone or not."

"I am quite certain that they did," I replied, "since the Justice Master held a strangling cord at the ready as he entered. It was only when I confronted him that he appeared surprised and produced his firearm."

Holmes nodded. "I think, as the door is now damaged, we will forego our intention to stay here this night. It is doubtful that we will see any more of our adversary, now that he knows he was expected. I trust you will be good enough to allow the three of us the convenience of one of your police vehicles when they arrive, Lestrade?"

"Certainly."

"Then I suggest that, until then, we discuss our future intentions. The Justice Master has had a narrow escape tonight, and we must ensure that his next encounter with us culminates, for him, with a meeting with the hangman."

Chapter 8 - Carpenters Mews and After

It was well after midnight when we entered our sitting room once more. We had first called at Miss Farrel's home in Hammersmith where, after she was safely inside, Lestrade had left a constable on guard. When I pointed out that she was now unlikely to be recognised, the inspector agreed but, for the time being, insisted on the precaution.

By now, both Holmes and I were weary. I did however, enquire of him before we retired:

"Has anything occurred to you, as to how we might progress further? I must confess that I am at a loss to imagine how we might proceed."

Holmes paused on his way to his bedroom. "We know, do we not, that the Justice Master is known at the Buccaneer tavern, by another name?"

"Mr Carvell has said so."

"And the tattooed man that Lestrade shot was also from there?"

"He was. We saw him when we sought out Mrs Porter."

"Precisely. It is there then, that our future enquiries are likely to take us." He turned the knob and opened the door of his chamber. "Good night, Watson. Doubtlessly we will have more to discuss tomorrow."

With that he was gone. When I sat down for breakfast the following morning, he was nowhere to be seen. The coffee pot had cooled, and our good landlady informed me that my friend had left more than an hour earlier.

A few days had still to pass before I was due to return to my practice, so I was free to spend my time reading and enjoying a long walk in the autumn sunshine around the streets of the capital. I ate luncheon alone, and only an hour remained before dinner when the front door slammed and quick footsteps ascended the stairs. Next moment a tall, tough-looking man burst into the room, the livid scar on his face prominent despite the fading light.

My service revolver is seldom far from my hand when we are engaged upon a case and I gripped it now, ready to draw it from my pocket as a warning.

"What do you want?" I asked the intruder.

"Some dinner would be agreeable, Watson, since I have not eaten since breakfast. You really should have become accustomed to my occasional changes of appearance, before now."

"Holmes! You are right of course, but I feel that my nerves are a little on edge since last night. Shall I ring for Mrs Hudson?"

He shook his head. "I can wait another hour I think, old fellow."

"Then, before you discard this rather brutal-looking disguise, perhaps you would care to tell me how you have passed the day."

"That is quite easily accomplished. I have been sweeping the floor and cleaning glasses in The Buccaneer tavern."

"They employed you?"

"After I convinced them that I am experienced in such work." He laughed. "I mentioned some fictitious inns in other parts of the country. They will never check my references, of course. I took the place of the tattooed man, whose name was Parker Mollet. To the surprise of his colleagues, he has not reported for work today."

"Nor will he ever," I commented unnecessarily. "do you intend to return there?"

"That would be quite without purpose," he said as he entered his room. "I have received my wages for the day, and the way to continue our investigation is now clear."

In little more than a few minutes Holmes returned, once more his normal self.

Mrs Hudson served our dinner shortly afterwards. Holmes ate slowly and continuously, apparently preoccupied with a review of his activities of the day.

I made no attempt to interrupt although my impatience at his silence was growing. Nevertheless, I was obliged to wait until the meal was over.

"It is quite evident that you are waiting for me to relate to you all that has transpired today, Watson," he said as we finished the last of our coffee. "The slightly vexed expression and frequent shifting in your chair are unmistakeable indications. I have no reason to go out again tonight, so I suggest we repair to our usual chairs, after which I will endeavour to satisfy your curiosity."

Our good landlady cleared away the dinner things as we seated ourselves, and for a short while we smoked cigarettes contentedly. Except for the rattle of passing traffic in Baker Street all was silent, and I was about to begin a conversation with the intention of guiding it along a path that would lead to the explanation I sought, when my friend blew out a final ring of smoke and stretched himself in his chair.

"There is not really that much to tell," he said then, "When I had convinced the rather bewildered fellow who seemed to be in charge of the running of The Buccaneer that he could expect a good day's work from me, my next task was to engage some of the others in conversation to learn what I could about the man we know as 'Vernon Stark'. As might be expected it was difficult at first, as they are a rather uncommunicative and solemn group, but after an hour or two I was able to get them to confide their various observations."

"He is a frequent customer, then?" I enquired.

"He consumes about half a bottle of dark rum, several times a week. One of the men whose job it is to manhandle beer barrels from the delivery carts to the cellar, told me that he considered Stark to have the smile of a lunatic, which goes well with Mr Carvell's description. Another fellow commented on Stark's birthmark, of which we have heard mention before, comparing its shape to that of a scorpion. None of this is of much assistance to our investigation of course, and I had almost given up hope of learning anything of significance when I chanced to be overheard in my enquiries by an unkempt elderly gentleman who has been a regular customer for many years."

"He contributed something further?"

"Indeed he did. He had formed the opinion that I was pursuing Stark because I was owed money, and was good enough to give me an address."

I raised my eyebrows. "That was fortunate. Where does Mr Stark live, pray?"

"On the outskirts of Cheapside, in lodgings at a place called Carpenters Mews."

"Doubtlessly, we are to pay him a visit."

"Of course, but not tonight. I am expecting another client in about," he consulted his pocket-watch, "half an hour from now. If you are not going out, Watson, may I suggest that you continue your reading. That is, unless you are interested in devising a remedy for marital squabbles."

I took my newspaper and medical journals to the table, to allow Holmes to use the chairs to interview his client as was usual for him. Apart from greeting a fine-looking woman with cascading black hair and rather aquiline features on her arrival, I took no part in the proceedings. It was unavoidable, however, that I should overhear the entire exchange, and the lady's problem seemed to be that her husband had left home a week ago after a quarrel. She had not heard from him since and a letter had arrived to tell her that he had taken his own life. Holmes asked the lady many questions, not only about their marriage but also concerning their friends and neighbours. She replied at length, and he listened attentively without interrupting before pronouncing that the situation was nothing more than a distasteful practical joke. He identified the perpetrator and told her that she would most likely find her husband in a hospital, after suffering an accident. He concluded by assuring her that he was available at any time, should his deductions prove incorrect.

When his client had departed I resumed my seat around the fireplace. "Holmes, I am always amazed when you solve these problems without leaving your armchair."

He shrugged his shoulders. "It was hardly difficult. When she explained her husband's disposition, I knew at once that he was highly unlikely to leave her for long. Her description of one of her neighbours, a Mr Spencer Beaumont, made it obvious that it was he who sent the letter, since he is infatuated with her and wishes her to leave for America with him. His intention seems to have been that they should depart before the husband reappeared, she believing that he had ended his life. An inconsiderate fellow, to say the least, since it appears not to have occurred to him that she would naturally require a certain time in which to grieve."

"She would be wise to avoid a man who would stoop to such measures, in any case."

"Indeed. And now, Watson, I see that it is getting late. I will see you at breakfast before I take a little jaunt to Cheapside, accompanied by yourself if you so desire."

With that he said goodnight and was gone. The door of his room closed softly behind him and I stared at it for several minutes before repairing to my own bed.

Next morning I arose to discover that Holmes had almost finished his breakfast. As I took my place at the table he put down his knife and fork and pushed his plate away.

"Ah, Watson, I fear that I have emptied the coffee-pot, but Mrs Hudson will doubtlessly bring another when she serves your meal. I can recommend the ham. Today, it is excellent."

As I ate, he commented on various articles he had apparently read in the newspaper which lay discarded near the basket chair.

"Are we to go to Cheapside," I enquired, at the conclusion of his observations.

"As soon as you have finished, if you are agreeable."

We set off shortly afterwards, in a hansom pulled by a young mare at a sprightly pace. Carpenters Mews was a tiny alcove off King William Street, where several plain but well-built houses nestled together. That many of these dwellings had once housed stables was clear to see, and after a cursory glance Holmes strode to the nearest and rapped upon the door with his stick.

"Number nine, if my informant was correct," he murmured as the door swung open.

We were subjected to brief but careful scrutiny by the middle-aged lady who confronted us. "Good morning, gentlemen. If you are seeking a room you have come at a fortunate time, since one of my tenants has left this very morning."

"Would that be Mr Vernon Stark?" I asked her.

She regarded me with astonishment. "Why, yes. But how did you know, sir? Are you friends of his?"

"Not at all," said Holmes. "In fact we have never met him. We are assisting Scotland Yard with an enquiry in which Mr Stark is likely concerned. My name is Sherlock Holmes, and my companion is Doctor John Watson."

"I see," the lady looked momentarily bewildered that the official force should wish to interview her former tenant, "but as I have said, he is gone. He left the week's rent he owed, but no forwarding address."

"That is most unfortunate. It will aid us greatly, however, if you will allow us to see his room."

"You may, of course, but I should mention that I have not yet had time to clean it. Mr Stark left hurriedly without all of his belongings."

I saw my friend's eyes gleam at this. "Did he give any reason for his abrupt departure?"

"He mentioned an emergency of some sort but did not elaborate, other than to say that he would not be returning. I imagine his haste was due to that."

"Had he been with you for long?" I enquired.

"Almost five years, I think. But come in, and I will show you."

We entered a pleasant hallway, and were led up a straight staircase to a landing boasting four doors. The landlady approached one and unlocked it, courteously standing aside to allow us entry.

"If I can be of further assistance, you have only to call."

Holmes thanked her and she descended as we closed the door behind us. For some moments he stood perfectly still and his head turned slowly as he took in the entire room.

I duplicated his action, but doubtlessly missed much that he observed. The bed remained unmade, the curtains hung half-closed, collar studs and a handkerchief lay on the carpet where they had fallen and the wardrobe door hung open.

"He was indeed in a hurry to leave," my friend confirmed. "The landlady stated that he departed earlier and she had not yet cleaned in here, but she must have entered since she was aware that Stark had left some of his possessions. It seems that, if he is the Justice Master, he may have decided to continue his activities elsewhere."

"The wardrobe contains some of his clothes."

"So I have noticed. It does not surprise me that they are of the sober colour and cut favoured by solicitors and the like, since I have suspected a connection to the legal profession from the first." He saw my questioning look, and smiled faintly as he explained. "How else did he know in advance the dates when his victims were to be released from prison? It is possible, of course, that he could have come by such information through a friend or acquaintance who is concerned with the law, so I could not be certain. Certainly, we have ample evidence that he had such knowledge before it was reported in the newspapers."

Holmes then examined the rumpled sheets, before getting to his knees to scrutinize the carpet.

"Clearly, this man does not smoke, and suffers violent nightmares," he murmured. "This whisky bottle that was concealed beneath the bed has been drained recently, since the spilled dregs have not dried or been removed by an otherwise conscientious landlady. Now, Watson, let us see what the contents of the wardrobe have to tell us."

"He has abandoned a pair of boots," I pointed out.

My friend withdrew them carefully. "From these, we can deduce that Stark favours his left leg, and has a noticeable limp."

"Because of the way the heels are worn down?" I ventured.

"Precisely. Also, his bootmaker, according to this label stitched inside, resides in Birmingham." He replaced the boots and drew out a hanger with a formal morning-coat draped across it. "Stark is left-handed, since the left sleeve is stained slightly with ink, and there are traces of hair oil on the collar."

"Not a fastidious man," I commented.

"Not concerning his appearance, at least. But what do we have here?" he plunged a hand into a pocket and produced several folded lists.

"Railway time-tables," said I.

"Indeed, and all but one have never been opened, as there are no creases. Apparently, Stark considered several destinations for his flight."

"But made his decision and consulted the appropriate time-table! What area does it cover, Holmes?"

He unfolded it. "The Midlands."

"Birmingham, perhaps, where the boots were purchased?"

"Doubtlessly that is where further enquiries will lead us. I think we will now return to Baker Street for luncheon, and to inform Mrs Hudson that we shall be away for a few days at least."

We thanked the landlady, whose name proved to be Mrs Adams, and took our leave. After a meal of Mrs Hudson's roast venison, we were about to repair to our rooms to pack a few things when the door-bell rang. A few minutes later, Mr Grantly-Knight was shown in.

"Forgive me, gentlemen, if I have disturbed your meal," he began, "but I am anxious to know of any progress you may have made towards identifying the subject of your investigation."

Holmes got to his feet and left the dinner-table. "Come in, Mr Grantly-Knight, and sit with us. I think you will find the chair before you to be the most comfortable. Would you care for tea, or a brandy, perhaps?"

Our visitor declined. "No, but thank you. I am here today because there have been rumblings within the Inner Temple. Gossip abounds that the criminal known as 'The Justice Master' narrowly escaped capture by yourselves and Inspector Lestrade." He paused as Holmes and myself took our seats opposite him, and smiled good-naturedly. "You did promise to keep me informed, Mr Holmes."

My friend nodded. "I can but apologise, sir. Events have taken several unexpected turns, and still we have nothing to show for our efforts. I take it that Lestrade, also, has neglected to enlighten you?"

"My work has prevented me from seeking out the Inspector, of late."

"Very well. I will now relate all that has transpired, until this moment. Then you will be as well informed as Watson and myself."

Holmes then proceeded to report our efforts towards apprehending our adversary. Mr Grantly-Knight listened impassively, his only animation throughout was a raised eyebrow as he heard of the Justice Master's escape in Brick Lane.

"And nothing has been seen of him since then?" he asked as my friend paused.

Holmes went on, I sensed with some reluctance, to tell of our suspicions of Vernon Stark, our visit to his lodgings and our intention of journeying to Birmingham in pursuit.

"So it would appear," our visitor concluded, "that something substantial has come of your enquiries, after all."

"It is not certain, but there is reason to believe so."

Mr Grantly-Knight considered for a moment. "At this time, I find myself in a rare and fortunate position. Withers, my clerk, has been absent for some little while with a fever, and I have therefore had no option but to transfer some of my work to my colleagues. The remainder I have just completed and, although I anticipate a very intricate affair to be forthcoming in the near future, there is currently an interval where I am able to enjoy some respite."

I glanced at Holmes, and saw a flash of anger in his eyes. My own feelings were of dreadful anticipation. We both knew what was about to be asked of us.

"What I am proposing," our visitor continued, "is that I accompany you gentlemen to Birmingham, so that I may see first-hand the capture of this Vernon Stark, if he is indeed the man that we seek. What do you say to that?"

"Is it not unusual," Holmes asked after a moment, "for a member of the legal profession to make such a request? Have you, perhaps, a personal interest in the apprehension of this man?"

Mr Grantly-Knight shook his head. "Not at all. The Justice Master has been at large for more than two years now and, besides yourselves, it is not only Scotland Yard that is anxious to see the end of his murderous career."

Holmes expression became thoughtful, and I assumed he was deciding upon a tactful way of rejecting our visitor's suggestion. Then, to my utter amazement, he smiled.

"According to my Bradshaw, our train will leave Euston in a little less than an hour and half. I suppose that will allow you sufficient time to pack a bag? Clothes for two or three days should be enough, I think."

Clearly, Mr Grantly-Knight was pleased by this.

"Thank you gentlemen," he said. "I will meet you at Euston Station in time for our departure."

With that he took his leave, and in moments Holmes and I were alone again.

Chapter 9 - The Next Victim

I still could not get past my surprise.

"Holmes, I am astonished!"

He turned in his chair, to look at me directly. "This has come about, I imagine, as a result of my permitting Mr Grantly-Knight to accompany us."

"It is most unusual, you must admit, for you to allow someone other than members of the official force to participate in our enquiries."

"That is so."

"Then why….? Of course, I see it now. You have mentioned that you suspected that this affair might be connected to the legal profession, and Vernon Stark's clothes suggested this also." I heard excitement creep into my voice as realisation dawned on me. "Do you suspect that Mr Grantly-Knight and Vernon Stark are the same person? Do you believe that he is the Justice Master? Have you consented to him being with us in order to observe his movements and actions?"

He smiled and held up his hands. "Watson, Watson, pray calm yourself. Your conclusion that I attach some suspicion to him is not entirely wrong, since his initial approach to us was instrumental in changing the course of our enquiries at the outset. It occurred to me at the time that he could be diverting us from the truth as easily as if he were assisting us to pursue it. We have encountered those whose intentions were to throw us off the track, before now. I, however, have not altered my original surmise that Mr Grantly-Knight seeks some personal advancement in his profession by involving himself in this affair. We shall see." He consulted his pocket-watch. "But time is getting short. Let us pack a few things, old fellow, and see where our enquiries lead us next."

Our travelling companion awaited us on the platform at Euston Station, dressed in dark travelling attire and carrying a single bag.

"Good day, gentlemen," he said in his distinctive voice. "According to the time-table, our train should arrive in ten minutes."

And so the journey began. Much to my surprise, Mr Grantly-Knight proved to be a conversationalist of some skill, and he was rarely silent throughout. My remarks were, by comparison, rare and those of Holmes rarer still, but my friend's sharp eyes seldom left the solicitor as the green fields and woodland flashed by.

In this way the hours passed swiftly, until we alighted in the early evening onto a crowded platform. Cages of racing pigeons stood stacked against the wall near the station master's office, and smoke billowed out as trains arrived and departed.

As we carried our bags through the arrivals hall, Mr Grantly-Knight glanced above us.

"I have read that New Street Station possessed a notable arched roof, and now I see that the description was not exaggerated."

I looked upwards. "Indeed."

Holmes did not reply. As we approached the pillars near the entrance, his gaze swept the street in search of a cab.

"Where are we to look for accommodation," I asked him.

"There is no need, for I have secured rooms by telegraph earlier. I regret, Watson, that no hotel awaits us on this occasion, but I am assured that our temporary lodgings will be comfortable."

"Near here, I assume?" Mr Grantly-Knight enquired.

Holmes raised his free hand and a brougham, evidently pressed into public service, came to rest before us. "Not so. We will be staying in a district called Winson Green, which is several miles away. However, I anticipate that we will arrive in time for supper."

"Surely, that is the name of the prison hereabouts?" our companion ventured.

"Quite so. The close proximity of our lodgings is precisely the reason that I chose them."

"We are to visit the prison, then?"

Holmes settled himself in his seat and waited until we had done likewise, before answering. "Such a visit would enhance our investigation, but I have not yet obtained permission. Tomorrow I will telegraph Inspector Lestrade to see if his influence extends to making a request to the prison governor on our behalf."

Little more was said and my friend gave instructions to our driver, who promptly set the horse to a fast trot. I looked around us as we left New Street behind and entered the long thoroughfare of Corporation Street, at this time busy with hansoms and the occasional landau.

"Theatre and restaurant traffic, I would think," said Mr Grantly-Knight.

"Undoubtedly," I replied, noting that Holmes was peering into the darkness expressionlessly.

We lapsed into silence again, the well-lit city streets giving way to dark suburbs which were quickly replaced by fields and skeletal trees. Leaves lay thick upon the ground, and in piles against the walls of isolated homes and small factories that loomed out of the night on both sides of the road. Then there were only buildings, a church here and there and stables, before we found ourselves among endless streets of terraced houses. Our driver guided the horse around several corners, halting in a poorly-lit street where most windows showed no illumination. He jumped down from his seat, and opened the door looking doubtful.

"72, Heath Street, gentlemen. That is the address you gave?"

"Indeed." Holmes stepped onto the pavement and handed the driver his fare. I followed with Mr Grantly-Knight and we retrieved our bags before the driver touched his cap respectfully and departed.

Holmes rapped upon the door and immediately the large window lit up. Moments later we were admitted by a round and jovial woman bearing an oil lamp, who promptly introduced herself as Mrs Hemstock and showed us to her dining-room.

The cuisine was every bit as enjoyable as that of Mrs Hudson, if a little less imaginative. We retired shortly after the meal was over, to find that our rooms were warm and clean. I formed the impression that our companion was used to grander accommodation, but he said nothing to confirm this. In fact, as we wished each other good night, both he and Holmes seemed to be in excellent spirits. For once I slept dreamlessly and without interruption, to awake to a fine autumn day.

Holmes left much of an excellent breakfast as he often did, causing Mrs Hemstock to be slightly bewildered. He went out while Mr Grantly-Knight and I had yet to finish our coffee, and returned as we repaired to the sitting-room to talk and smoke. We were about to settle ourselves as he joined us, producing his old briar and lighting it from the fire with a spill.

"We probably have an hour or two to wait," he informed us as he exhaled smoke in a cloud. "Lestrade may be engaged elsewhere upon a case, or be fully occupied at the Yard. However, he is not a man to hesitate, when he gets the scent."

Our companion threw the remains of his cigarette into the fire. "Do you anticipate that Lestrade will be able to arrange for us to visit the prison today, Mr Holmes?"

"I have every reason to expect so. I made it clear in my message that to delay could cost Alwyn Randall his life."

Mr Grantly-Knight and I looked at each other in bewilderment, and then at Holmes.

"Who is…?" I began.

"Alwyn Randall is another reprieved prisoner," Holmes explained. "Unless I am mistaken, he is the reason for Vernon Stark's presence here. As soon as I had ascertained where he had fled to, I made enquiries with Scotland Yard as to the release dates of any local prisoners who were previously condemned. Randall is the only release from Winson Green for the next few months."

"What was his crime?" asked Mr Grantly-Knight.

"He was convicted of killing his infant son, but there was always doubt. During the last ten years there have been several campaigns to free him and one has finally succeeded. He is elderly now and quite infirm I understand, factors which may well have assisted in securing his release."

"When does he regain his freedom?" I enquired.

Holmes looked at both of us with a faint air of amusement, anticipating how the answer would be received. "At four o'clock, this afternoon."

He could not have been disappointed, for Mr Grantly-Knight and I looked at each other in surprise. Neither of us had suspected that time was so short.

"Doubtlessly you will appreciate that Stark is now more likely still to be the Justice Master," Holmes resumed. "I cannot believe that his coming to Birmingham and Randall's release are coincidental."

Mr Grantly-Knight shook his head in a hopeless gesture. "But what can Stark possibly hold against an elderly man who has been in prison for years?"

"There is nothing. There is no sense, rhyme or reason to the selection of his victims. Primarily they are prisoners who have escaped the hangman, but it seems that they also qualify who impede his purpose or threaten it in any way. There is no other possible conclusion: the man is mad and totally without remorse."

"So, if we are successful, he himself will face the hangman," said I. "Or he will spend the remainder of his days in an asylum."

"In either case," Holmes agreed, "he will not be at large on the streets of London or any other place, ever again."

Such was the conversation between us throughout the morning. Holmes had refilled his pipe twice and Mr Grantly-Knight smoked half the contents of his cigarette-case, before a telegraph boy rang the door-bell.

Moments later, Mrs Hemstock entered after knocking our door politely. "This has arrived for you, Mr Holmes. If you gentlemen are agreeable, I will serve luncheon in half an hour."

We indicated that we would attend the dining-room then, and she left. Holmes tore open the yellow envelope that he had plucked from her tray.

"Lestrade has secured an interview with the prison governor at two o'clock," he read aloud. "He does not seem to have great faith in our line of enquiry, but he has contacted the official force hereabouts and informed them of it. They are insisting on sending their own man to accompany us to the prison. We will meet Inspector Bradnell there at ten minutes to two."

We repaired to the dining-room, where Mrs Hemstock produced a gigantic cheese and potato pie. When we had eaten our fill and dealt with the dessert and coffee (Mr Grantly-Knight would take only tea), I consulted my pocket-watch.

"The time for our appointment is fast approaching, Holmes."

"I am aware of it. Do not concern yourself, old fellow, we will be punctual."

"But there are no hansoms in the street."

"We shall have no need of one."

Mr Grantly-Knight rose from the table. "Let us retrieve our hats and coats, and walk among these charming streets, then."

We ignored his sarcasm, if that was what had been intended, and strolled along Heath Street in the opposite direction to that which had brought us here. The terraced houses were small but, almost without exception, maintained well. Once or twice we noticed movement in the windows as we passed. Curious observers quickly retreated behind spotless lace curtains.

"Gentlemen are an uncommon sight hereabouts apparently," Mr Grantly-Knight concluded.

Holmes and I said nothing for, with the gradual bend now behind us, we were confronted by the grim façade of Winson Green prison.

"Doubtlessly, the fellow in the bowler hat and long brown overcoat is Inspector Bradnell," Holmes said.

"He looks rather downcast," I observed.

"The detective division do not normally receive outside intervention with good grace," Mr Grantly-Knight commented. "It is viewed as needless interference."

Holmes and I glanced at each other and I caught his quick smile. We knew well the truth of our companion's remark.

We crossed the street and introduced ourselves to the taciturn Inspector, who proved to be humourless and spoke only when it was essential for him to do so. He hammered on the prison gates and this brought an immediate response. A panel slid aside and we were admitted after a short exchange. The gates closed behind us and the atmosphere of desolation descended upon us at once. I felt my spirits sink as we were led across the cheerless exercise yard and into the building. This place, after our earlier visit to Holloway, was already causing a depressing effect.

The guard who accompanied us gave our names to his colleague, who sat behind a desk in a dreary office. Names were crossed through in the ledger before him, and we were directed to proceed. After a succession of corridors, we came to a heavy door on which the guard rapped with his fist. A faint acknowledgement from within allowed him to usher us in and announce us.

"Come in, gentlemen," the man behind the ornate desk bade us as the guard withdrew. "I understand that you wish to see me regarding the prisoner Alwyn Randall, who is to be released in," he glanced at the longcase clock in the corner, "just under two hours."

Inspector Bradnell, who evidently knew the governor, made the introductions and said little else during the interview. When we were bidden to sit upon hard, stiff-backed chairs, he alone elected to remain standing.

"My name is Cullen," the governor began. "I have read of you, Mr Holmes, and marvelled at your many successes. I cannot escape the impression however, that Doctor Watson has leaned toward the sensational in his depiction of them."

"I assure you, Sir, that my portrayals of both events and those concerned with them are entirely accurate." I said in an affronted tone before anyone else could speak.

I immediately regretted my outburst, for an embarrassed silence settled upon us.

"We are here to prevent a possible murder," Holmes said to restore the conversation.

The governor raised his eyebrows. "Here? In this prison?"

"No, but we have reason to believe that Randall will be in considerable danger on leaving here. With your permission, we would like to remain here until his release, so that we may accompany him to a place of safety."

Mr Cullen stroked his carefully-tended beard, probably reviewing Holmes' request for contradictions with prison regulations. During this short interval I allowed my eyes to rove around his office, although there was little to distinguish it. A portrait of our Queen hung on the wall behind the desk and a framed photograph, presumably of the governor's wife and family, stood near his large and unmarked blotter. Apart from the desk and chairs, the only furniture was a rather battered coat-stand in a corner.

"I see no reason why we cannot oblige you," he concluded at last. "But I am curious to know who could possibly wish harm to Randall. He is elderly and not in good health, and I have my doubts that his new-found freedom will benefit him for long."

"There is a madman at large," Mr Grantly-Knight interrupted. "He appears to kill released prisoners who he believes should have hanged. We strongly suspect that he is here in Birmingham, and nearby. That can only be to claim the life of your prisoner."

Holmes' irritation at the solicitor's interjection was apparent to me, but he said nothing.

After a moment of apparent confusion, the governor's expression lightened. "There is a criminal who calls himself the Justice Master," he said then. "I have read of him. Is it he who we are discussing here?"

Holmes nodded. "He is deceptive and resourceful, and I am determined that he shall face the very justice that he claims to represent. My plans are in place to apprehend him,"

I saw a scowl appear on Inspector Bradnell's face. Although Holmes and his methods were now well accepted by much of the official force in and around the capital, I reflected that this had yet to come about in more distant parts.

Mr Cullen looked at the clock again. "Very well. You have not long to wait. I wish you well with this."

Promptly at four o'clock, a guard that we had not seen before met us in a dismal corridor near the entrance. He was accompanied by a frail white-haired man of obviously advanced age, who was immediately transferred to the custody of the guard who had awaited us during our interview with the governor. Few words were exchanged, and as we approached the gate it was opened at once. The guard retreated silently as we regained the street.

Nearby, a rather shabby coach pulled by two grey mares waited.

"We have provided transport, as Inspector Lestrade requested," Inspector Bradnell said tonelessly. "I will leave you now, gentlemen. Good day to you."

With that he turned abruptly and strode away, to turn a nearby corner and vanish from our sight.

"Unfriendly fellow," I remarked, but Holmes and Mr Grantly-Knight were already approaching the coach with the silent and stumbling Randall. In a moment, we were seated and the coachman urged the horses onward.

Randall stared at each of us in turn, and then spoke for the first time. "Where are you taking me?"

"To a place where you can be protected," Holmes informed him.

"You have no right to abduct me. I am now a free man."

"Indeed you are, but you are not aware that your life is in danger. When the threat has been dealt with, you may go wherever you wish."

Randall looked confused. "But I have no enemies. Who would wish to harm me?"

Holmes introduced us all, and explained about the Justice Master.

"This man must be mad," Randall concluded.

Holmes nodded. "I am quite sure of it. But you must see the peril that almost certainly lies ahead for you, unless you remain under our protection."

"If things are as you say, then I have little choice. I suppose I should be grateful."

"That is something that you must decide for yourself. Pray obey my instructions at all times, and we may well prevent further loss of life."

Randall appeared to sink into deep thought, while Mr Grantly-Knight and myself were keen to learn from Holmes about the arrangements he had apparently made.

My friend consulted his pocket-watch. "You have doubtlessly realised that we are returning to New Street Station," he said then. "The time is now fourteen minutes past five o'clock, and our train leaves at half past the hour. By my calculations, we should arrive with minutes to spare, and once we have boarded I will tell you what lies ahead."

Mr Grantly-Knight peered out of the window, as he had several times. "Mr Holmes, I believe that we are being followed," he said with some agitation.

"I should be surprised if we were not," Holmes replied. "That hansom you see back there has been out of sight for only brief periods since we left the prison. It may contain the Justice Master or an agent of his whose task it is to determine our destination, which we will not attempt to conceal because I intend that this time he shall not escape. When he strikes, we will be ready."

Chapter 10 - Plantain Castle

We had hardly settled ourselves when the train began to move and the station was quickly left behind. I saw that Holmes had observed intently the crowd waiting upon the platform, but no one appeared that he recognised or to whom he seemed to attach any suspicion.

The smoking-compartment that he had reserved (I concluded that he must have done this, along with other arrangements, some little time ago, and must therefore have deduced the direction that the case was likely to take) held the faint aroma of tobacco and of leather, and we easily made ourselves comfortable.

He and I sat side-by-side, with Mr Grantly-Knight and Alwyn Randall occupying the long seat opposite, as the train gathered speed and the factories and houses of the city gave way to fields of dull grass and trees with naked branches.

"I really do think, Mr Holmes," said Mr Grantly-Knight, "that you might confide in us as to our destination. After all, we are unaware even of the length of the journey."

"According to my Bradshaw, we will have travelled 162 miles when we reach the end of our journey," was the reply. "It will take us, I estimate, less than four hours."

"But where are we bound for?" I enquired.

"We are about to spend a day or two in a charming village, or so I am informed, called Great Rutley. It is near the south coast and lies three miles from Dover."

"Is our accommodation arranged?"

The ghost of a smile crossed Holmes' face. "Have no fear, Watson, we will not be sleeping beneath the stars tonight, nor will we be wanting for sustenance. Some years ago I was able to be of some small service to Sir Roger Merestone, the owner of Plantain Castle. The keep is now uninhabitable, but there is a solid hunting lodge that should meet our needs adequately. The area is rarely visited these days, for Sir Roger and his family have taken up residence elsewhere."

I can recall little else of the journey, except that Mr Grantly-Knight, Randall and myself slept for part of it. I awoke several times, usually during a brief halt at a station, to find that Holmes had remained wide awake with his position unchanged.

There were some intervals of conversation between us, mostly about the current political situation and, surprisingly, some of Randall's experiences as a prisoner, during the last forty miles. Then the train began to lose speed and the sparse light from several oil lamps illuminated the signs proclaiming our approach to Great Rutley Station.

When all motion had ceased we took our luggage and left the train. A rotund and elderly station master hurried along the darkened platform towards us with an oil lamp in his grasp.

"Are you Mr Sherlock Holmes, sir?" he asked my friend.

"I am he," was the reply.

"Sir Roger has sent a trap, sir. It awaits you in the lane, near the entrance."

Holmes surrendered our tickets. "How far is Plantain Castle, do you think?" he asked.

"Two miles, sir, no more. I pass it every day as I ride here on my bicycle."

"My thanks to you."

The man saluted as we made our way past the waiting room and ticket office, before entering a long tree-lined lane. All was darkness, the bare branches appearing indistinctly - skeletal fingers reaching towards a moonless sky as we approached the conveyance that awaited us. A man in dark clothes turned to us from lighting the lamps.

"Good evening, gentlemen," he greeted us as he took our bags. "My name is Thomas. Sir Roger bids you welcome and has said that I should confirm to you that all has been made ready."

We murmured our thanks and climbed aboard. There was ample room and we seated ourselves on long benches without difficulty. The journey was not unpleasant, since the winter coldness had not yet set in, but comprised of a succession of ghostly avenues of trees and empty fields. We spoke little throughout, silently watching as dark silhouettes appeared and faded. Once or twice the cry of an animal or bird was heard briefly.

At last we turned into a wide gateway, where one of the stone animals, rampant atop the posts, had crumbled. Thomas brought us to a halt and we alighted.

"The castle, or what remains of it, stands further along this drive, gentlemen," he explained, "but the path that you see to your right leads directly to the hunting lodge. I will accompany you with some of your luggage, and return for the remainder when you are settled. If you would care to follow me…"

He made to set off along the path, but Holmes placed a hand on his shoulder. "Thank you, but there is no need. We will carry our bags, while you return to Sir Roger. Kindly convey to him my thanks, for his invaluable assistance."

Thomas passed his lamp to my friend. "Very good, sir. It shall be as you say."

We watched as the trap passed out of our sight, and then picked up our bags and set off. The land sloped gradually downward before us, and after a while the moon emerged from the clouds to reveal our surroundings more clearly. Less than a quarter of a mile to our left stood the remains of Castle Plantain, a shapeless hulk that appeared as a darker patch against the night sky. The only inhabitants now would be roosting birds, but it had an eerie air that could be felt even from a distance, and I remembered reading in a periodical that bloody battles had once been fought there.

"We are almost there." Holmes said after a short while. He pointed ahead, to where a square stone structure was dimly illuminated by moonlight.

I took note of its position and saw at once his reason for selecting the place for our purpose. It stood alone in a natural clearing, with rising land at its back and about three hundred yards of open field before the dense trees of a small forest began. The building could not be approached other than openly, concealment was clearly impossible.

As we neared the door Holmes withdrew a key, which I presumed that Thomas had given to him, from his pocket. It turned with difficulty in the ancient lock and the hinges squealed as the door opened. We stepped inside and he used the light from his lamp to seek out others, which he lit until the room was filled with illumination. I looked around me and saw that the place was not unpleasant. I reflected that, especially during my army service, I had known much worse.

"It will no doubt suffice," said Mr Grantly-Knight.

"This place suits me more than prison," Randall murmured with approval.

We bolted the door and proceeded to settle in. It was arranged that Holmes and Randall should occupy the two tiny bedrooms to the rear of the lodge, leaving the more spacious living area to Mr Grantly-Knight and myself. I was grateful for this as close confinement is abhorrent to me, although I have had to put up with much of it, over the years. I confirmed that the two long couches would serve as comfortable beds, and sought out warm blankets to see us through the night.

Randall surprised us all by, after inspecting the food which had been left for us, producing a meal of fried eggs and toast. We ate hungrily, and spent an hour in conversation before tiredness overcame us. We repaired to our sleeping-places after Holmes had warned us to be on our guard constantly.

"But we have seen nothing as yet to suggest that the Justice Master has followed us from Birmingham," I pointed out.

"You yourself saw no one on the platform as we departed the station, Mr Holmes," Mr Grantly-Knight reminded him. "I constantly observed our fellow-passengers during the journey, as I am sure you did, and there seemed to be no one who could possibly be our adversary."

Holmes nodded. "I also considered that the Justice Master may have some skill at disguising himself, and therefore scrutinized our travelling companions closely with the same result as yourself. However, I noticed on arrival the time-table on the notice board near the station master's office. A further train, travelling an identical route to that travelled by ours, was due to arrive in Great Rutley two hours later."

I consulted my pocket-watch. "So, he could be here, by now."

"If he is as astute as I believe, he will have discovered our whereabouts, probably by representing himself as a colleague of ours to the station master, and be either close by or on his way at this moment. I suggest that we avail ourselves of a good night's rest, and be prepared for whatever tomorrow may bring. I do not think that we will be in doubt of his presence for long."

Long after retiring I lay awake, fully dressed. The only sounds, apart from Mr Grantly-Knight's heavy breathing, were the distant lowing of cattle. Once I heard a frantic squeak, possibly the death-cry of a vole or field-mouse becoming prey to an owl, before a shallow sleep finally came.

I awoke with a start, half-remembering the loud noise that had dragged me from my slumber. Then a tremendous crash came again and I sighed with relief, for I recognised it as nothing more than a clap of thunder. Sudden rain beat upon the windows, followed by lightning that lit up the room for an instant and renewed my anxiety at once.

Mr Grantly-Knight was nowhere to be seen!

I waited for the next flash, and in that brief interval saw that the bolt on the door had been drawn. It crossed my mind that perhaps Holmes' early suspicions had been correct after all

– had the Justice Master been in plain sight, accompanied us even, from the beginning of this affair?

Then I heard the door of my friend's bedroom opening softly, and in a moment he stood beside me, his ear-flapped travelling cap already on his head.

"He has not been gone long," he whispered. "Like yourself, I remained dressed. Put on your hat and coat and ensure that your service weapon is to hand."

I obeyed and we crept out into the open air. The sky had cleared, heavy clouds retreated as we watched, and moonlight again bathed our surroundings. Holmes locked the door and gestured for me to remain as he encircled the building and viewed the land behind it, before reappearing from the shadows and speaking quietly:

"There is no sign of him near the lodge, and nothing to conceal him beyond. He can only have entered the woods."

At Holmes' indication we moved away from each other, so that we could come upon the trees from different directions. I pressed forward stealthily, losing sight of my friend as the trunks and leafless branches separated us. My eyes adjusted to the deeper blackness and I inclined my head in a bid to hear movement ahead. From where I estimated Holmes to be came not the slightest sound, but my blood seemed to freeze in my veins as I heard a horrible gurgling sound together with the noise of a desperate struggle.

"There, Watson, just ahead. Quickly!" The shadowy figure of Holmes burst out of the closely-spaced trunks to my right, moving with the speed of a running deer. I followed as best I could, so that we reached a small clearing, thickly carpeted with shrivelled leaves, at almost the same moment.

I felt the beating of my heart grow faster, and a tightening of my nerves as he lit his dark lantern to reveal the writhing figure of Mr Grant-Knightly lying before us and covered in blood. A cruel gash extended across his throat, and in his agony he tried to speak to us.

"Weather," he seemed to be saying in a choked whisper. I could only assume that he connected the attack he had suffered with the recent lightning storm in some way, but could not imagine how. He continued to make a valiant attempt to communicate as I fell to my knees to be of what assistance I could, but from the first I knew that it was hopeless. I had hardly drawn near to him when he gave a final shudder and expired, with agonised words still upon his lips.

I got to my feet and shook my head. Holmes face was grim in the poor light.

"We shall probably never know how he was lured here without first raising the alarm," he said. "But at least, thanks to him, I now know the identity of the Justice Master. We must cover the poor fellow with leaves to conceal him as best we can, until arrangements can be made." He was suddenly very still. "No, that can wait until later. Watson, I have been a fool – we must return to the lodge at once. Run as you have never done before."

He hurriedly extinguished his dark lantern, then turned and rushed back through the trees with extraordinary speed. The urgency of it (for I had instantly discerned his fears) seemed to give me the strength to stay near to him and I fancied that his revolver was in his hand. My weapon also was at the ready as we left the trees behind us. With much effort we increased our pace further as we gained the distance to the lodge. Drawing closer, we heard the shattering of window-glass and saw a fiery cloud blossom within.

"He threw an oil-lamp into the lodge," Holmes shouted. "Try to bring him down, Watson, while I attempt to bring Mr Randall out of there."

Already smoke was billowing from the shattered window. I could see the flames flickering fiercely and casting grotesque shadows, and a surprised cry from within turned to a scream. Holmes was struggling with the lock and I heard the door crash back on its hinges as he disappeared into the inferno. Just beyond the glow I saw movement, and a shadow flittered like a bird in the darkness.

"Stop!" I cried. "Halt at once or I will fire."

The reply came instantly in the form of a fusillade. I threw myself to the ground, feeling the moist earth against my hands and the side of my face as the bullets whined overhead. The thud of footfalls grew fainter and I raised my head to find that nothing confronted me but the long, untended grass and bushes that formed a screen-like barrier ahead.

I got to my feet warily. The night was silent except for the crackling of the fire some way behind me. Holmes appeared beside me, although I had not heard his approach. I could smell the fire on his clothes.

"We must move from here, Watson. The blaze behind us makes us an easy target."

As we altered our position, I asked him: "What of Randall? Is he safe?"

"He is unharmed, apart from having suffered a severe shock followed by a prolonged coughing fit. The oil lamp was thrown into the room that you and Mr Grantly-Knight occupied, so it was simply a matter of avoiding the spreading flames for long enough to enter the inner chamber to drag our charge out." He peered into the undergrowth before us. "Remain here with your revolver at the ready. If our quarry emerges he will look first at your former position. Take him prisoner if you can, but if he attempts to fire upon you do likewise at once."

With that he melted into the darkness. I was glad of the reassurance of my service weapon as I held it pointed at the tall vegetation, estimating where the Justice Master had entered its concealment. I strained my eyes and my ears, but learned nothing. The sounds from the burning lodge were now much reduced, probably because the building was constructed mainly of stone. Then a bird, suddenly disturbed, flew up with a startled cry an instant before the grass was forced apart by our adversary emerging at a full run with his firearm ready to discharge.

"Put down your weapon!" I cried, but he raised it on hearing my voice. I do not know if I could have pulled the trigger before he was able to fire but it proved unnecessary, as Holmes appeared from the bushes beside him and delivered a blow with the barrel of his revolver. The Justice Master sank to the ground, his firearm lost.

"I was fortunate enough to find an accessible path through the undergrowth," Holmes explained. "My progress was impeded by the need for silence, but it seems I arrived in time."

"Indeed, you did." I approached the prone body, a man not unconscious but with his arms enfolding his head. I saw that there was little blood, except for a stained bandage around his wrist that could have been the result of our previous encounter, and that my attentions were likely not required. Nevertheless, I grasped his wrists and pulled him to his feet, revealing his countenance by the light of the moon and the remaining glow from the lodge. "This man is unknown to me, Holmes."

"Then allow me to introduce you to the Justice Master, otherwise Mr Charles Withers. You will recall that Mr Grantly-Knight mentioned his clerk, once or twice."

It struck me at once that the word I had heard as 'weather' was actually Mr Grantly-Knight telling us that he had recognised his assailant, and I was glad that I had not shared my conclusion with Holmes. "You have said before now that your suspicions were with the legal profession."

My friend lit his dark lantern. "Either that or our adversary had friends there who confided in him. How else could he have known in advance of the release of prisoners formerly convicted of serious crimes? Really, Watson, you have every right to be ashamed of me – I should have realised the truth of this the moment Mr Grantly-Knight mentioned that his clerk had been away from his employment because of illness. I fear that I am guilty of a severe lack of reasoning."

I was about to object when I saw in the poor light that our prisoner's eyes had focused. A furtive expression crept onto his face, and he grinned at us in a way that reminded me of a schoolboy, caught out of class as a truant. Here was a man who in no way resembled my preconceived impression of our enemy – he was of no more than average height, pale-faced and bald (the wig had moved when Holmes struck him, revealing a livid birthmark) and evidently left-handed, from the way he had held his pistol.

"Well, it appears that you gentlemen have me at last," he said.

"It was not an easy matter," Holmes admitted. "But I am curious as to why you embarked on this murderous path. I have not encountered many men who would kill without reason."

Withers seemed to consider for a moment. "Except madmen, no doubt. But you must not think me mad, for my purpose will become clear to you. The hangman awaits me I know, so there is nothing to be gained by concealment."

"Then pray continue."

"I do not know if you are familiar with the lives of those I have dispatched," he looked from Holmes to me and seeing no confirmation, continued, "but the first of these was the woman Martha Berryfield. During her courtship she discovered that the man who was to be her husband was wooing another woman also. She sought out her rival, befriended her and poisoned her, leaving no obstacle to her forthcoming marriage. Her victim, who was quite unaware that she shared her suitor, was my beloved sister. Berryfield married and subsequently disposed of her husband, again using poison on discovering his further faithlessness. When I read of her arrest and imprisonment I welcomed the news, for she had never been brought to trial for the murder of my Cybil. I followed the proceedings by means of the newspapers, anxious to learn that she would pay the penalty, but Viscount Ferrersly intervened. His lawyers were the most skilful in the land, and I am certain that the Viscount would have regretted greatly his employment of them, had he realised that his trust in his wife was misplaced. It was she who was conducting liaisons with the husband of Martha Berryfield and she who, in a curious onset of conscience, indirectly secured Berryfield's release."

"I have observed the strange ways of the fair sex before now," Holmes commented. "The Viscountess felt responsible, as she was the cause of Martha Berryfield's anger towards her husband which culminated in his murder. It was these events then, that encouraged your desire for vengeance?"

"At first it happened only in my mind, a fantasy, but after a while the notion dominated my thoughts. I would imagine Martha Berryfield walking freely, enriched by her husband's wealth and uncaring that she had put my Cybil in her grave. I tell you, gentlemen, I all but gave up taking in sustenance, some days consuming nothing but a glass of dark rum, as the hate within me became an obsession. I resolved to mete out the justice that the law had failed to administer. There could be no wrong in this, for my intended victim had murdered at least twice and the courts had allowed their judgements to be swayed by persuasive tongues."

"Your intention here is at least understandable, if not lawful. But why did this not end there? What reason could there be for you to seek other victims?"

Withers hesitated, then shrugged his shoulders as he answered Holmes' question. "For days after Martha Berryfield lay dead, the memory of what I had done filled my mind even while I slept. How many others, I asked myself, had been cheated of their rightful revenge by the very law that should have exacted punishment? It came to me that I could secretly restore the balance, impose such justice that had been denied the public by the undeserved clemency of our failing courts. I set about making my plans for correction."

"Thereby becoming no less guilty than your victims," I pointed out.

"Perhaps, but what was I to do? To rid the world of these unpunished souls had become my mission in life, the need to act was like a thirst – a fire in my blood."

"Not all those that you have murdered had committed any crime," Holmes reminded him. "How can you justify that, even to yourself?"

Withers' face became expressionless, a strange glint shone in his eyes. Finally, he shook his head. "Some were a threat, I could not countenance interference or the possibility of the law bringing my purpose to a premature end, while others were simply in my way. I cannot say that I feel any regret for being the instrument of the demise of any of them – the urgency of my crusade was such that I could not tolerate obstacles. However, I find myself profoundly sorry that I will no longer be able to pursue the course that I have accepted as my destiny."

Holmes and I glanced at each other, each appalled by our prisoner's callousness.

"How did you entice your employer, Mr Grantly-Knight, from the safety of the lodge?" I enquired then. Withers stared at me momentarily as if he had failed to understand the question and, indeed, I was never to hear the answer, for at that moment I heard someone hurrying towards us. Mr Randall, wearing his nightshirt with a coat thrown around himself, appeared out of the darkness and called to us:

"Mr Holmes, Doctor Watson! Are you safe? I heard gunfire."

Holmes and I turned towards him and instantly realised our error. Withers sprang away in that moment of distraction, limping to disappear once more into the dense bushes and tall grass before I could raise my revolver. Holmes returned the police handcuffs that he had been about to place on Withers' wrists to his pocket, and warned Mr Randall against advancing further.

"Stay back!" he cried. "If you value your life." He turned to me. "Watson, keep your weapon ready. It seems that our night's hunting is not over yet."

We entered the thick growth warily, our weapons held before us. Holmes had extinguished his dark lantern so as not to give Withers an indication of our position, and the tall stalks that surrounded us cast wavering shadows in the moonlight.

"Slowly, Watson, with caution," he whispered, as we crept forward glancing in all directions.

Suddenly I felt my friend's steely grip on my shoulder, and was still instantly.

"Step back, at once," he hissed urgently and I complied, momentarily confused until I realised that here the foliage ceased. Ahead of us was only impenetrable darkness, and I formed the impression that the ground fell away abruptly.

"Holmes, we almost stepped over the edge."

"As Withers has already, apparently. Surprisingly, he did not cry out, but he must have fallen since there seems to be no concealment nearby. It is time to return to the lodge, I think, or to whatever is left of it. In the morning we will know more."

So it was that we accompanied Randall back to the burnt-out remains of our shelter. We were fortunate in that enough of the lodge had escaped the flames to still afford us some small protection from the elements, and that sufficient food remained to provide a simple breakfast.

We ventured out, leaving Randall in the shelter, soon after first light. After retracing our steps of earlier we stood again at the place where the undergrowth gave way to a sparse patch of land that terminated in a yawning abyss.

"Doubtlessly an ancient sea once beat against this headland," Holmes surmised," for the hillside for about a hundred feet below has been significantly eroded. Observe, Watson, that the muddy track beneath shows no sign of disturbance, so Withers must have fallen onto a ledge that is invisible to us from this point. If we turn our heads and incline ourselves slightly however, we can see the continuation of no less than three such ledges far off, from where it would be a simple matter to climb either back up or to descend to the track beneath. That, it appears, is how Withers made his escape and he is therefore still at large. I confess that I expected to see his body displayed below, and to some disappointment at our failure to apprehend him." He turned away abruptly and hurried me back through the foliage. "We must make haste back to the lodge, since Mr Randall is still in danger."

Chapter 11 – Lestrade Closes the Case

Our concern for Randall proved needless, and we proceeded to arrange our departure. Plantain Castle, I thought, appeared no less menacing in the clear morning light, and I confess to little regret as we left the locality behind. We carried that of our luggage that the fire had spared for about three miles by my estimation, but I was by no means certain of my assessment. As we emerged from what seemed like a network of narrow lanes, I hailed a passing cart and secured assistance from the farmer's boy who drove it. He was kind enough to deposit us back at Great Rutley Railway Station, at the promise of a half-sovereign. We caught the early train.

Holmes was not in good spirits during our return to the capital, so such conversation that took place was mostly between Mr Randall and myself. I must say that, now he had become accustomed to our company, the ex-prisoner proved to be unexpectedly adept at conducting a lively discourse.

We arrived at Victoria Station and Holmes immediately surrendered our tickets and led us quickly out to the nearest waiting cab. At Scotland Yard he sought out Lestrade, but on learning that the inspector had been called to Limehouse on a matter connected to a disturbance in an opium den, he promptly approached Inspector Hopkins. The details of the case and of our activities were impressed upon him by my friend, who then wrote out a full account and requested that Lestrade be informed upon his return. Hopkins assured us that this would be done, and further promised that Mr Randall, who was to be left in his charge, would be afforded the protection of the official force until the Justice Master was finally captured.

Upon our return to Baker Street Mrs Hudson, who had somehow anticipated our reappearance as often before, served our luncheon as soon as we had refreshed and seated ourselves. I was glad to partake of the chicken pie that steamed before us, having eaten little at breakfast. Holmes ate with indifference, and I knew that our failure to bring the murderous career of the Justice Master to an end still troubled him. When the meal was over we repaired to our armchairs, where he sat with his head tilted back in deep thought until he shook himself like a wet animal. Freed from his recollections, he appeared to have resolved to temporarily put the affair aside.

"Well, Watson, I cannot see that we can do anything more until some further development presents itself. I have asked that Scotland Yard inform us at such a time, and that they keep a watch on any prisoners convicted of serious crimes at their release until Withers is finally in custody. Until then, I suppose I may as well turn my attention to anything else on hand."

From time to time I looked up from my perusal of the medical journals that I had allowed to accumulate, to see Holmes considering the contents of letter after letter before casting them aside. At length he selected one, and sat smoking his old briar in silence until he rose from his chair to peer out of the window. When twenty minutes had passed he suddenly laid down his pipe after knocking it out, then ran like a madman from our room and down into the street. He returned wearing a satisfied expression.

"I did not hold out much hope of seeing any of the Irregulars pass by, but my timing was fortunate. I have sent a message to Wiggins, and he will be here with a couple of his lieutenants before too long."

"That will not please Mrs Hudson," I reminded him. "You will recall that she has given permission for Wiggins alone to enter our lodgings, and not often."

"Quite so, but I observed our good landlady leaving to buy food, as I watched the street."

"She may return, and then you will be scolded like a schoolboy."

"That is unlikely to happen. You see, Watson, she was carrying the canvas bag that she uses exclusively for her purchases from the butcher's in Carradine Street. It is a fine day and so she will walk there, and I am thus able to accurately estimate the time she will be away. I shall ensure that our visitors have departed by then."

I smiled at the outraged vision of Mrs Hudson that appeared in my imagination, and announced that I also was about to go out. Holmes made no objection and I therefore concluded that he had no immediate need of me, and so spent the next half hour wandering the nearby streets and peering into shop windows.

"Payment will be at the usual rate, plus a bonus for whoever actually discovers the whereabouts of this man. Wiggins, you will report to me your findings, and you will do so alone."

These were the words I heard on re-entering our room. As I was about to close the door behind me three urchins filed past. Each, to my surprise, politely acknowledged that I had hesitated to allow them to pass. I heard them take the stairs at a run, before slamming the door loudly.

"Let us hope that they obtain the information you need, Holmes."

"I have every confidence that they will. It promises to be an unusual problem."

And so began the affair that I will one day publish entitled 'The Adventure of the Artificial Cockatoo', if I am so permitted. Otherwise the misadventures and difficulties of Mr Septimus Craig will forever remain recorded only in my despatch box.

It was by now nearing dinner-time, and we talked for a while of one of Holmes' former clients who, according to the mid-day edition of *The Standard,* had recently passed away.

Once more, I ate with relish. Holmes consumed his beef medallions with more interest than before, and I was glad to see this. Faced with a new case, his spirits seemed to have lifted.

When Mrs Hudson had cleared away our plates we once more seated ourselves around the fireplace where, with a little prompting, my friend related to me an intriguing tale which, to my regret, I will never be able to share. Our conversation was interrupted only once during the evening, when an unexpected telegram arrived. Holmes glanced at it with disdain, before tearing it to pieces and consigning it to the waste-paper basket.

"Not from the Justice Master?" I enquired, remembering some of the previous communications from that source.

He shook his head. "Some people, it seems, are far from conversant with the function of a consulting detective."

From this I gathered that the telegram had contained a totally inappropriate proposal or request, such as I had known Holmes receive from time to time. It is true however, that some of these had quite unexpectedly blossomed into some of his most unusual cases, but he had long become adept at extracting the pointless and the ridiculous.

As time wore on I became weary, and my friend was quick to notice this. We finished our port and retired. Once abed I listened for the sound of Holmes' pacing, which he often did in the midst of an unfinished case, but nothing disturbed the silence. I drifted into a dreamless sleep.

The following day saw the conclusion of the Septimus Craig affair. Wiggins made his report and received payment as promised. Holmes had drawn his conclusions without leaving our rooms. Little else transpired, as we were confined to our lodgings by heavy rain for the remainder of the day and the next. I finally read the last of my medical periodicals and Holmes brought his index up to date.

The conclusion of our unfinished investigation was to take place the day after, when breakfast was over and Holmes had made a fruitless search of his post.

"Nothing new, Holmes?" I enquired while looking down from our window.

"Your observation is correct. An invigorating walk, I think, would be the best way to spend the morning. The midday post may bring something of interest."

"We may have to postpone our excursion. Inspector Lestrade has just arrived in a hansom, and is heading in our direction with a spring in his step."

My friend raised his eyebrows and we sat in our armchairs to wait. A moment later the door-bell rang and Mrs Hudson announced our visitor. The inspector looked unusually pleased with himself, smiling as we exchanged greetings.

"Would you care for a cigar, Lestrade?" Holmes asked when we were seated.

"I don't mind if I do, Mr Holmes."

Holmes extracted them from the coal-scuttle and we all smoked, the air quickly becoming tainted with their fragrance. Lestrade's pleasantness was somehow unnerving.

For a little while the conversation comprised of meaningless enquiries about each other's health, from which nothing resulted that Holmes would not have already observed. A moment's silence was swiftly concluded, as my friend's impatience became evident. He said suddenly:

"You are looking very smug today, Lestrade. I perceive that you have something to tell us."

"Could it be," I interjected, "that you have new information concerning the Justice Master?"

The inspector ground out his cigar, appearing more pleased than ever. There was a touch of triumph in his demeanour. "I have indeed, gentlemen. I am glad to announce that Scotland Yard has brought the case to an end."

Holmes finished his own cigar and leaned forward in his chair. "Excellent. Pray enlighten us."

"Certainly, and with pleasure. After I brought a case in Limehouse to a successful conclusion, I returned to the Yard to find that Hopkins had left your report on my desk. I was as disappointed at Withers' escape as you must have been, but it occurred to me that further examination of the area surrounding Plantain Castle might be to some advantage. I therefore took Sergeant Morely and two constables down to Great Rutley yesterday on the mid-day train. Fortunately the rain there had ceased, and our investigation proceeded well."

Here Lestrade paused, I suspected for effect. While I was anxious to hear of his findings, Holmes sat patiently and impassive.

"In fact, we learned much." Lestrade, I could see, waited for Holmes' response. He was disappointed.

I, however, could not bear the uncertainty. "You have evidently been very thorough, inspector. Do continue, your account is most interesting."

"Thank you, doctor." He glanced at Holmes with something like disappointment. "We carefully examined the hill top. I say that, but it is more like a steep cliff, where you say the Justice Master escaped by rushing through all that wild grass and disappearing over the edge. Like you, I saw that the muddy path beneath was undisturbed. My conclusion therefore, was that Withers had found a way across those dangerous ledges that run all along the cliff face and was either hiding somewhere near or had reached the point where it was possible to descend. I had no hesitation in ordering Sergeant Morely, who has mountain-climbing experience on Mount Snowdon, to lower himself down using the ropes for which I had anticipated the need. When he stood upon a ledge, from where he could see much more of his surroundings, I told one of the constables to secure the rope and stay with it, while the other constable accompanied me on the long walk that took us to the place where we could approach the path at the bottom of the cliff."

"When you came to the point where the sergeant had been lowered, what did you discover?" Holmes asked.

"I looked up and saw that he stood with his back against the cliff face, appearing shocked. There is a small cave on that ledge, and I could see someone who appeared to be suspended in the air glowering down at me. We got back up to the top as fast as we could, I can tell you, and pulled Morely up. I wanted to hear what he had to say, before proceeding further."

The inspector interrupted his narrative, I suspect to regain his breath as he had become rather excited. There was an atmosphere of expectancy in the room, and Holmes wore a knowing expression which I found puzzling. A dull silence was complete, except for the rumble of passing carriages along Baker Street and the occasional movements of our landlady as she immersed herself in early preparations for luncheon.

"What did you learn from him?" I enquired then.

"He said that the sight that confronted him caused him to cry out, such was his astonishment. This was confirmed by the constable above who by then had become concerned. The sergeant had quickly realised that he was not alone on the ledge, for a few feet away a hideous spectacle faced him. A man who answered the description in your report perfectly, Mr Holmes, glared at him with wild eyes and a mouth hanging open as if crying out in agony. He had jumped from the clifftop to the ledge, not seeing the pointed tree stump in his path because of the darkness."

"He had impaled himself," Holmes said.

"Exactly, but the stump was drenched with blood, and Withers must have died in great pain. Sergeant Morely was quite shaken. Surprisingly, for he is not without experience.

We then retrieved the body by means of an attached rope, and I made suitable arrangements for its return to London after we had done so."

"And so," I said somewhat unnecessarily, "the Justice Master will murder no more."

Smiling, and in a hearty fashion, Holmes jumped to his feet. "Lestrade, I am overjoyed for you! You have brought this case to a final and absolute conclusion." We all rose and he seized the inspector's hand and shook it vigorously. "You presented me with this affair, yet it turned out that you had no need of my assistance. My congratulations, sir! I am quite certain that Doctor Watson feels similarly."

"Indeed I do," I concurred, rather taken aback by Holmes uncharacteristic response to Lestrade's account. "An admirable piece of detective work, and an example to your colleagues."

"The official force has its uses, gentlemen," the inspector remarked with a trace of embarrassment. "But the Yard thanks you for your assistance in this matter. However, it was only a matter of time before our methods would have proved too much for Withers, in any case." He took out his time-piece and glanced at it briefly. "But now, having informed you of the outcome of this affair, I must return to the Yard for an interview with the Assistant Commissioner. Likely he has summoned me to offer his congratulations also. Perhaps promotion is in the wind, who knows? Allow me to thank you again, and wish you both a very good morning."

With that, Lestrade took his leave of us. As the door below closed I became aware that Holmes was struggling to contain his mirth.

"What has amused you?" I asked him.

"Lestrade has had a bad time of it, these last few months," he replied as he regained his composure. "Gregson snatched the credit for solving the killings at the Rendezvous Club from under his nose at the last instant. Also, both the kidnapping of Mrs Romilla Lester and the scandal that has been brewing at the Stock Exchange remain unsolved. It is good to see the inspector in good spirits, after the increasing melancholy that has possessed him of late."

I gazed at him critically. "I know you, Holmes. Something is amiss here. It was apparent to me the moment I saw your face during Lestrade's explanation."

"Then tell me, old fellow, what did you deduce from such a meagre indication?"

He looked at me expectantly, a half-smile playing about his lips. I took a moment before answering, to assemble my thoughts so as to give him the least chance to enjoy himself at my expense. From outside the angry voice of a passing constable floated up to us rebuking, it seemed, a beggar or troublesome urchin.

"I first became suspicious," I began, "as you made out your report at Scotland Yard. It struck me that you went to considerable and unnecessary trouble to prevent me from reading the contents. Add that to your extraordinary actions and expressions during the inspector's visit, and I am forced to the conclusion that you instructed him precisely how to deal with the remainder of the Justice Master affair in such a way that he would believe that he alone had solved the case." I put a hand to my brow as something further occurred to me. "I remember also my puzzlement when you failed to examine the cliff face from below, the morning after Withers escaped us."

Holmes clapped his hands and laughed. "Watson, I have said before that we will make a detective of you yet. However, I see that luncheon cannot be more than a half hour away. You have not made any plans for this afternoon, I hope, since I have a surprise for you. There is to be a violin recital at St James Hall, and this new Austrian is highly-praised in the entertainment columns. The tickets await us there, and I am sure we can be dressed and in attendance by half-past two."

Also from Arthur Hall

In addition to the six books in the Rediscovered Cases series, Arthur is a regular contributor to the MX Book of New Sherlock Holmes Stories – the world's largest collection of traditional short stories.

Arthur has released two collections of those same stories as separate books.

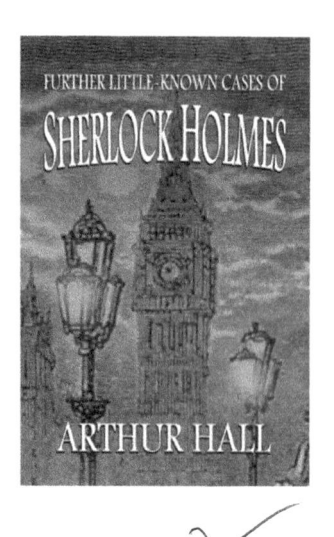

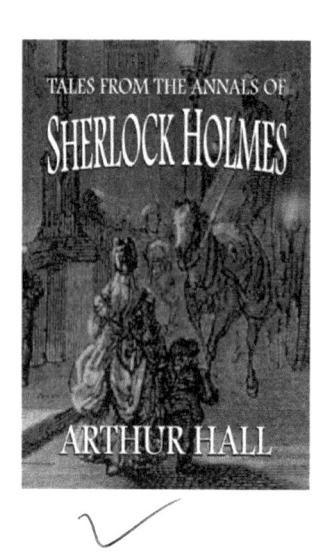

Further Little Known Cases of Sherlock Holmes and Tales From The Annals of Sherlock Holmes. You can see all Arthur's books on his profile page:

https://mxpublishing.com/collections/sherlockian-author-profile-arthur-hall

Also from MX Publishing

MX Publishing is the world's largest specialist Sherlock Holmes publisher, with over a hundred titles and fifty authors creating the latest in Sherlock Holmes fiction and non-fiction.

From traditional short stories and novels to travel guides and quiz books, MX Publishing cater for all Holmes fans.

The collection includes leading titles such as *Benedict Cumberbatch In Transition* and *The Norwood Author* which won the 2011 Howlett Award (Sherlock Holmes Book of the Year).

MX Publishing also has one of the largest communities of Holmes fans on Facebook with regular contributions from dozens of authors.

https://www.facebook.com/BooksSherlockHolmes

www.mxpublishing.com

Also From MX Publishing
Traditional Canonical Holmes Adventures by
David Marcum
Creator and editor of
The MX Book of New Sherlock Holmes Stories

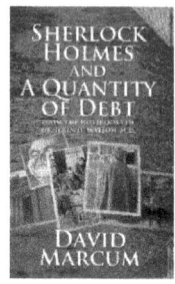

The Papers of Sherlock Holmes

"The Papers of Sherlock Holmes *by David Marcum contains nine intriguing mysteries . . . very much in the classic tradition . . . He writes well, too."* – Roger Johnson, Editor, *The Sherlock Holmes Journal,* The Sherlock Holmes Society of London

"Marcum offers nine clever pastiches."
– Steven Rothman, Editor, *The Baker Street Journal*

Sherlock Holmes and A Quantity of Debt

"This is a welcome addendum to Sherlock lore that respectfully fleshes out Doyle's legendary crime-solving couple in the context of new escapades . . . ." – Peter Roche, Examiner.com

"David Marcum is known to Sherlockians as the author of two short story collections . . . In Sherlock Holmes and A Quantity of Debt*, he demonstrates mastery of the longer form as well."*
– Dan Andriacco, Sherlockian and Author of the Cody and McCabe Series

Sherlock Holmes – Tangled Skeins
(Included in Randall Stock's, 2015 Top Five Sherlock Holmes Books – Fiction)

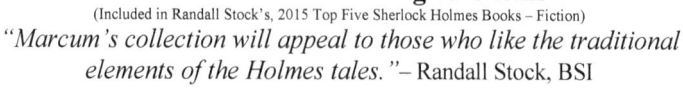

"Marcum's collection will appeal to those who like the traditional elements of the Holmes tales." – Randall Stock, BSI

"There are good pastiche writers, there are great ones, and then there is David Marcum who ranks among the very best . . . I cannot recommend this book enough."
– Derrick Belanger, Author and Publisher of Belanger Books

150

Also from MX Publishing

Our bestselling books are our short story collections;

'Lost Stories of Sherlock Holmes', 'The Outstanding Mysteries of Sherlock Holmes', The Papers of Sherlock Holmes Volume 1 and 2, 'Untold Adventures of Sherlock Holmes' (and the sequel 'Studies in Legacy) and 'Sherlock Holmes in Pursuit', 'The Cotswold Werewolf and Other Stories of Sherlock Holmes' – and many more……

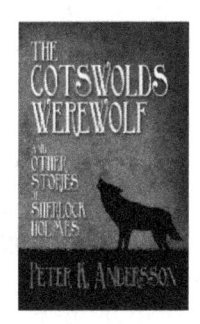

www.mxpublishing.com

Also from MX Publishing

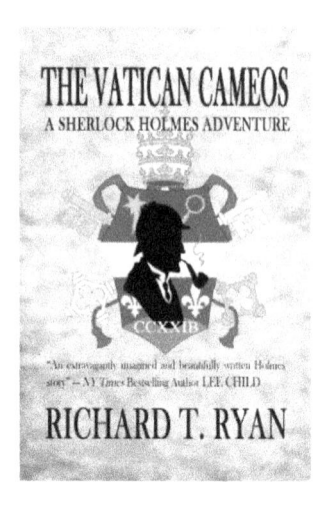

THE VATICAN CAMEOS
A SHERLOCK HOLMES ADVENTURE

RICHARD T. RYAN

When the papal apartments are burgled in 1901, Sherlock Holmes is summoned to Rome by Pope Leo XII. After learning from the pontiff that several priceless cameos that could prove compromising to the church, and perhaps determine the future of the newly unified Italy, have been stolen, Holmes is asked to recover them. In a parallel story, Michelangelo, the toast of Rome in 1501 after the unveiling of his Pieta, is commissioned by Pope Alexander VI, the last of the Borgia pontiffs, with creating the cameos that will bedevil Holmes and the papacy four centuries later. For fans of Conan Doyle's immortal detective, the game is always afoot. However, the great detective has never encountered an adversary quite like the one with whom he crosses swords in "The Vatican Cameos.."

"An extravagantly imagined and beautifully written Holmes story"
(**Lee Child**, NY Times Bestselling author, Jack Reacher series)